THE ORPHAN FROM SPACE

M. L. HUMPHREY

THE ORPHAN FROM SPACE

Published by Virgo eBooks Publishing
4800 Basin Harbor Rd,
Vergennes, VT, 05491, USA
www.VirgoeBooks.com

January 2014

Formatting: Virgo eBooks
Cover design: Marius Epure

ISBN 13: 978-0615955254
ISBN 10: 0615955258

Contents

PREFACE

Situated between the fourth and fifth planet of a yellow star on the outer arm of our galaxy, is a ring of debris consisting mostly of rock and dust that never formed a planet. Some of it is residual, dating to when the planets were formed, the rest being captured space debris that wandered the universe until being taken in as a stray. The rocks have three main classifications based on their composition, carbonaceous, silicate, and metallic.

For the last three months a survey ship from the planet Evenset of the Pansonett system, far closer to the hub of this galaxy, has been examining how this ring of debris was formed hoping to learn more about how the development of this part of the spiral galaxy differs from its opposing arm. Did both arms develop equally in the beginning and diverge as they aged, or is there some truth to the present convention that they are equal in all aspects.

Living within this survey ship are three families working together, living together, and raising their children side by side. These are exceptional people, with exceptional skills, just making a living doing celestial research for grant money.

CHAPTER 1

"Dora? What are you listening to?" I asked. The little twerp was perched on her bunk with her eyes glued to a small viewer.

"Butt out brother, none of your business" was all I got out of her.

I just wished dad hadn't found how to decode the broadcasts from this systems third planet. He had been searching through the spectrum looking for any sign of Queryl when he ran across these signals. It took him about three days before he was able to separate the video and audio components and recreate the original broadcast. Dora had gotten hooked on several of the shows, as they were called, and whined until he had setup a full, almost real time satellite feed for her to watch. To do that, someone had to post a receptor satellite in the planets orbit. Arial got to do that while I got to sulk about it.

I told him it was a waste of time, but he said that "learning their language and what life was like for them was useful knowledge." So dad declared that we had to learn the language and the way life on this planet the inhabitants called Earth. In particular, the United States, as broadcasts from other parts of the planet were not as strong.

I was reluctant, but Dora dove in like a person obsessed.

Mom was a little reserved about it as were the others, but it beat the everyday boredom for a while. Especially now that we were hooked up to a large asteroid we have affectionately labeled Alpha-1.

My name is Jasom, and we are the Kingston family; Harkinson and Valya are my father and mother. Oh, did I mention the twerp? That would be my younger sister Dora, she is the impossible one but I guess we'll keep her. However, we were not the only people aboard the "King's Quest", there are seven others. The Haldon family consists of Arson, his wife Jayla, and their two daughters, Arial and Selda. Then there's the Janon family, Charnon, his wife Parma, and their 8 year old son Tomer.

Mom and dad were the oldest and the major stake holders in the ships operations. Arson is almost as old as dad, and the titular captain as well as head of communications. His wife Jayla is the expert in biologics and in charge of the hydroponics and anything else dealing with plant life and food; both incoming and outgoing; if you know what I mean. Both Charnon and Parma were in charge of the engines and supplies. They were much younger than the rest of the adults. Dad's the person in charge of operations and mom's the geologist.

As for the children, Arial is nineteen, four years older than I am, Dora and Selda were ten, and little Tomer eight. As you can see, Tomer and I were greatly outnumbered by all of the older women. It was probably the only thing we had in common.

Tomer was a quiet little child with a full head of blonde hair just like his father. He also had inherited his father's quietness, quite the opposite from his mother who was so very outgoing.

Dora and Selda both had brown hair worn short and claimed they were sisters. But underneath I could see that Dora was destined to be the outgoing one and Selda the quiet scholar.

Now Arial, on the other hand was not only the oldest, but was also the bossiest. An energetic bundle of red hair and enthusiasm, and I endured her because I adored her; and she knew it. There must be some saying somewhere that would fit her, but for now she was just Arial, spoiled child and rotten to the core, and I loved her.

Our ship was one of many family ships that wandered between the many star systems searching for knowledge, mainly for academic reasons as these excursions were fully funded by several of the colleges and universities throughout the known systems. We all speak Wessar, a language that has its roots in the dark ages of our culture and is still being spoken today. Some say it was the language of the predecessors, but most people doubt that.

We operate on grants and other types of funding as we roam the cosmos searching for knowledge and clues of that unknown race of people that had traveled throughout the stars thousands of years before us; we simply call them the 'Predecessors'.

There is little left of the Predecessors, no artifacts other than an occasional derelict ship, and so far we have learned very little about them. The ships that have been found, have been nothing but bare hulks and completely empty. Analysis of the ships environment leads us to believe that they were oxygen breathers much like us and about the same physical size and shape.

Some people even thought that they were us and that at some long ago time something had happened and we, as a civilization, had slipped all the way back to barbarism on a small world near the farther end of our spiral galaxy. It had then taken over two millennia for our people to climb from that barbarian stone age culture back to plying between the star systems.

When we found the first abandoned space ship, orbiting an empty planet, we thought there were other people out there. The phobiacs were positive that they were inimical and that we should pull back to our own world so as to avoid notice. Cooler heads prevailed and after finding only three other derelicts there were no more indications that there was anything else out there; that is until we met the Queryl.

The Queryl were another race of beings from somewhere nearer the center of the galaxy. All we know about them is that they are chlorine based, look like monsters, and their ships are not as fast as ours. Truth be known, no one has ever really been in contact with a Queryl or ever seen one. When faced with capture their ships disintegrate leaving nothing to make any assumptions about. Analysis of the composition of the dust left over shows a high level of chlorine, oxygen, nitrogen, and selenium. For now we just try to avoid them.

Periodically our family ships would meet on our home world of Evenset in the Pansonett System. A gathering is where many of the family run ships would gather to trade, tell stories, and swap people. Not every group of people can live together in such a small space and get along well, so a means of swapping family groups helped to keep things sane.

CHAPTER 2

"Harkinson, dear" mom called as dad was returning from working on Alpha-1. "Have you seen the latest reports on Queryl today?" she seemed a little agitated. "I fear they may be getting close."

"Nonsense" he replied jovially, "I've been watching the indicators and we haven't seen any markers that they're heading this way."

"Arson?" he hollered to the man on the radio watch, "Queryl update please!"

"Sure, checking now." There was a short pause as Arson cycled the instruments and read out the results. "There are some disturbances, but I can't tell if it's just noise from the gas giants or where it's coming from."

"Thanks Arson, heads up" dad called back to him.

"Aye aye" he laughed.

"Well Valya, we've got a good one here, the deposit has turned into a vein that follows around the back side. We should be able to get several thousand pounds of ore over the next week" as dad sat down in the rec room. Dora was in the corner still watching one of the programs beamed up from Earth.

"She even talks like an earthling dear" mom replied, "sometimes I can't tell if she's really ours or not."

"You telling me, that a wandering asteroid miner might be her father?" he replied with a smile.

Parents, sometimes I don't understand what they're talking about.

But tomorrow I would get to do my own survey for the first time. I had been combing over some of the survey data that Arson had been accumulating before they had tied off to Alpha-1. Some of the data suggested there might just be a load of another very valuable element just a couple of rocks over. I had convinced dad that it was time I did a survey on my own. I couldn't wait.

"Jasom, dear" mom called from outside my hatch, "I need a hand with the classifier, it will only take a moment."

"I was just getting ready to head out to the latest target mom, can it wait?" I replied.

"No dear it would be best if we did it now."

"OK mom, be right down." It was right on the way, just stop in, fix the classifier, and head down to the hanger access.

I left my suit and helmet on the bench outside the hanger access and stepped into mom's territory. As she was head mineralogist, she relied on her equipment to gauge whether it was worth the expense of extracting whatever ores or minerals we found. The asteroid we were working at present had an almost pure streak of Dutorium that, if it continued, would make the whole trip highly profitable. Telemetry had found a trace of Orcium on another object not far beyond it and I wanted to try my hand at surveying it.

"There you go mom, there was just a little dust in the mechanism. Have to keep it clean to work right."

"Thank you dear" she replied, "and where are you headed?"

"We have a trace indicator of Orcium on an object just beyond this one. I want to see if I can find anything else. I won't be long."

"Keep your channels open and remember the safety procedures. I wouldn't want to scrape my only son off a cold rock. I would be very mad at you for that."

Her icy gaze brought a hasty "Yes Sir" as I hurriedly backed out of her lab and headed to the hanger access.

This wouldn't be the first time I've taken the flyer out on my own, both mom and dad had insisted on many training flights and many, many hours of examinations before I was allowed on my first excursion outside, away from the family ship. I could literally fly this thing with a blindfold on.

"Preflight checks OK, radio communications OK, AWX-01 ready for flight" I sent to Arson sitting up in the communication center.

"AWX-01 ready for flight, confirmed. Safe flight Jasom, keep in touch. Report every ten minutes."

"Every ten minutes confirmed, AWX-01 away" I replied hitting the eject button. The launcher responded by pushing the flyer away from the ship's side. Not far, just enough to give it some maneuver room.

Flyers, as we called them, were actually miniature spaceships, easily handled by a single good pilot. They had sufficient storage for cargo and up to four people, but were not meant for long trips. After three or four days, the recycled air and water would not be pleasant. Besides, some things could only be washed and scrubbed so many times as certain nutrients just couldn't be replaced.

I checked the status indicators, all OK as I set the response timer for ten minutes.

Slowly the flyer moved ahead of the ship so I could get a look at the target. I kept the recorder running as I fed a little boost into the forward thruster and the flyer moved slowly across the sunny-side edge of our mining operation toward the darkness beyond.

"Time to engage auxiliary lighting" I said to the recorder while keying the controls to bring the mirror into play. To use it properly I had to stay in the sunlight and focus the beam into the darkness behind Alpha-1.

I had to be careful as the beam only illuminated a small part of what was hiding in the dark. No, I wasn't afraid of monsters or anything like that, but the asteroid belt was a constantly shifting mass of boulders and other rocks that could grind a small flyer to bits if you weren't careful. This massive shuffle of rock and dust was the result of the varying gravitonic forces caused by the nearby planets orbits. Nothing was static out here.

Watching the indicators and what was visible in the reflected light was hard. The mapping screen would show where everything was, but not what it was. The indicators could discern what they could from the reflected data beam. But my eyeballs still liked to see what it really looked like.

"Ping!" The indicator has found something. I gently coaxed the light beam onto the area marked on the mapping screen. Nothing showing yet, have to get in closer and investigate.

"Be-ep!" the timer went off, time to make the ten minute report.

I punched the report button and spoke into the recorder what I had found so far with a short comment on further action. Anything I did would have to be from the cockpit of the flyer, nobody went out alone. "Waiting for response before continuing" as I hit the button again for transmit. Procedure was to wait for acknowledgement and comments before commencing any further actions.

"Hold there son" dad called back. Then he quizzed me on all of the steps I'd performed and what I intended to do next. "Very good Jasom, remember to stay inside the flyer and be back in twenty minutes."

"Yes dad, AWX-01, continue, confirmed."

I fed a little more forward thrust to come in closer to the spot that the indicator had a hit on. Slowly the light ahead of me darkened as the flyer moved into the shadow of Alpha-1. I was now on instruments until I was close enough to turn the lights on.

"Tick, tick, tick, tick-a-tick, tick-a-tick, click" the change to click was a warning to stop. I fed a little reverse thrust and brought the flyer to a halt about a hundred feet from the edge of the target.

I let the scanner make multiple passes and assemble a composite of what it could find on the surface. I didn't realize how much time had gone by when I heard the "Beep" of the timer again.

Again I punched the recorder and gave my findings as well as my return route. This time I fed a little upward thrust to return to the sunshine where I could use the mirror again while waiting for confirmation of report findings.

This time it was Arson who replied.

"Nice report Jasom" he replied, "got some good materials we can really use in there. I've passed it down to Valya for verification, wait for her confirmation before returning.

"Wait for confirmation before returning, check!" I replied.

Might as well see the sights while I wait, I thought. Slowly I swung the mirror across the object I had been studying; it wasn't much to look at. With each swing I started raising the mirror to look further behind it.

Wait! What was that? I stopped the mirror and slowly backed it up. There, a flash of light, or a reflection? It was a reflection, the flash happened only when the light was shining on it.

I keyed the recorder and fed a little forward thrust keeping one eye on the reflection and another on the mapping screen.

"Jasom?" mom's voice caught me off guard, "where are you going?"

"Switching to live feed" I replied, "found something that reflects light, directly ahead. Advise?"

"Hold your position son" dad called, "let's see what's out there first."

"AWX-01, holding." I replied feeding a slight amount of reverse thrust to halt forward motion. "AWX-01 hold confirmed" I intoned.

"What are you up to out there kid?" a young girls voice chides me. Arial is a few years older but I still think of her as younger.

"I'm holding Arial."

"Arial!" Arson bellowed, "Get off the circuit.

"Yes daddy" was all I heard before there was a loud click.

"Jasom, I'm coming over" he called, "stand ready to assist me."

"Yes sir" I replied. Mom and dad boss me around, but Arson is boss outside the ship.

I didn't have to wait long before the little explorer came into sight over the top of Alpha-1. Unlike the flyer, it was a machine made specifically for mining; its multiple arms and appendages could fasten onto an object and literally tear that object apart. It had just the one seat for an operator and that only big enough for his space suit.

"Can you give me a bearing and distance Jasom? I can't see it from here."

"You're going to have to come right down in front of me; it's at the end of a long corridor of moving rocks. I have a distance of 1.34 standard."

"Acknowledged, commencing movement" as Arson moved the little machine down in front of the flyer and pointing down the line of sight bearing I had just given him.

"Got it! Hold your position Jasom, I'm going around a different way" as he swung the explorer up and over the intervening asteroids.

A few minutes later he called back. "Jasom, I'm going to shine a light down into the rocks over here. Let me know when you see it."

I stared down the slowly closing rocky corridor looking for his signal. There it was. "Mark, I see it. It's a little further out, maybe a couple of hundred feet more."

"Check" Arson replied. "Let me know when you see it again."

I kept watching and then he found it. "Right there!" I yelled. "What do you see?"

He didn't respond for a bit, but the light stayed on the object in question. Maybe it was an illusion I thought and turned the mirror a bit. No he was right there, I could see the light moving around.

"Jasom, did you turn off your light?"

"No sir just moved it a little, I'm setting it back now." as I swung the mirrors light back down on the object again. "It won't last much longer though, the asteroids are closing up. It was a good thing he hadn't tried to go down that corridor of rocks.

"Jasom, I've got it marked, you head back to the ship now."

"AWX-01, return to ship, confirm" I replied.

"AWX-01, return to ship, confirmed" dad confirmed from the other end. I stowed the mirror and headed back.

CHAPTER 3

I couldn't make up my mind whether to hang around the hanger access waiting for Arson to return or to head up and see what dad was doing.

"What are you doing Jasom? You do know where the freshers are, don't you?"

Arial had snuck up behind me; she could be so exasperating at times. Maybe that's why she interested me so. Dora was just plain obnoxious, but Arial was pleasant to look at. Her bright red hair was cut short to fit into her helmet which of course was under her arm. It was her shift to take the flyer out.

"I'm waiting for Arson to get back. I found something out on the back side of our rock and he went out to investigate."

"Then they sent you back here." The last was with a sly smile. "I know all about it."

"Is that where you're going?" I accused. I couldn't believe that they'd let her out there and not me. Sure, she's older, and she's Arson's favorite daughter. Actually, he treated her more like a son.

"Don't worry kid" she knew that rankled me, "we all know who actually found it, and when it turns up to be a can, we'll all know who to blame." She smiled with that last taunt and plunked her helmet on.

I glowered at the flyer hatch as it closed behind her and again at the warning buzzer, time to vacate the hanger bay. A can is an object that uses too many resources to find out it's worthless.

I headed down the corridor to the rec room and dropped into a vacant chair still glowering. A too familiar slap on the back of the head snapped me back to reality.

"Stop that ,twerp!" I yelled at Dora. One of these days, one of these days I would get even.

She dropped into the chair opposite me and gave me a stony stare back. No matter what I said she had never been afraid of me. As well as being my little sister, this little bundle of energy was almost my alter ego.

"I bet it's Arial again." was all she said.

"What's Arial?" I grudgingly replied.

"Any time you're in a bad mood it has to do with Arial." Her expression didn't change for a moment, than with a wan smile "you know she really doesn't care for you that much."

"Umph" was all I could manage.

"She's cruel, self-centered, and general all around

spoiled rotten by that no good father of hers." she stated with an impish grin.

Now she was making fun of me. My face must have exposed my boiling frustrations for she sat up straight and just returned my stare. Then again, somehow she always managed to smooth out my wrinkles.

"If I don't smooth out your wrinkles, who will?" she said as if reading my thoughts.

"I've got to stop telling you my inner secrets, twerp, you're starting to read my mind."

I twisted around in the chair trying to get comfortable.

"There's more, isn't there" she probed.

I broke down and told her what I had discovered. That I was peeved to be brought back so others could go out and do the actual discovery. I should have been the one out there instead of her, working with Arson. "She told me it was probably just another can and I would be to blame."

"Can or not, if Arson was intrigued enough to spend more than five minutes with it there must be something there. It was probably mom who had you brought in; you know how mothers can be."

Her banter was beginning to cheer me up.

"Jasom?" the intercom bellowed, "where are you?"

"In the rec room mom, Dora and I are just talking."

"I don't hear any screaming?" I almost laughed; mom had a very dry sense of humor.

I heard some mumbling before she continued. "You will want to be up here for this, Arson is sending back video." Then there was the click of the closed connection in the empty rec room.

I was quick, but Dora beat me out the door and up the hall to the comm. center.

Once inside there wasn't much room as everyone else was there as well.

"What did we miss?" Dora wanted to know.

I wisely let her do the talking, she could prod mom so much better than I could.

"Nothing yet, they've just got the camera unpacked and powered up. OK, here it comes." The room got very quiet as the view screen lit up with a black and white image of Arson sitting in his little explorer.

"OK, can you read me? Hold the camera steady Arial."

"Good center, good focus Arson. What have we got in there?" dad commented.

"Well, it's a little hard to tell for sure, but I think we've found a derelict. The hull is intact, lots of scrapes and buried in debris." He replied as he turned the explorer and motioned for Arial to move the flyer into position where we could get a look at it.

"How buried is it?" Dad asked. "Could we do an extraction?"

"Arial, a little more to the left. Rotate ten degrees to

the right...good. Hold it right there while I shine the light."

Slowly we could see down amongst the rocky outcrops the general outline of a derelict. It looked like there were several layers of boulders floating in between; that would not be an easy pull to extract it.

"Hmm" dad murmured, "I don't think we can get close enough to do much. You're closer Arson, what do you think?"

"I'm not saying it isn't possible, but it's going to be difficult and it's going to take time. Lots of time we may not have" he replied. "I wonder..."

"Can't we call for help?" Dora burst out.

"Arson?" dad demurred, "Your thoughts?"

"I was thinking along the same lines. I don't think we've got what it's going to take. We should probably just tag it and leave it. Is it worth an instagram?"

An instagram was a highly directional, high speed communication, sent through a wormhole. It took a lot of power to set it up and a very accurate directional bearing. The further away your target, the less chance of it getting there.

"Have you been able to identify the class of ship, any hull markings?" Dad asked.

"I'm going to drop a drone down, stay connected, shouldn't take too long, I had Arial bring one out with her."

We waited nearly an hour while they dropped the drone down through the debris field. Arson used the controls to record every angle of the field around it before setting it in a course to completely map the exterior. Mom was recording both feeds while Jayla monitored their vital signs.

"Check, drone has just finished mapping, I'm bringing it back up. Arial, stow the camera and pull back out of the debris field. I'll be right behind you."

"Arson!" Jayla called, "you're at the end of your nominal out time, start picking up and heading back. Arial, mind your heart rate and follow him back."

"Agreed, when we get back we're going to have to make some quick decisions. There's more to this then what we've just seen" was his cryptic response.

With that he pulled the drone in and attached it to the side of the explorer and pulled up beside the flyer. He motioned for her to go first and followed close behind.

Mom and dad exchanged a strange look. I don't think anyone else saw it, but Dora poked me and we snuck out the hatch and back down to the rec room. It would be most of an hour before they got back and stowed all their equipment.

CHAPTER 4

By virtue of getting there first, we had the prime seats in the rec room for the big meeting. Not everyone was in here, as there had to be two people always on watch, one for communications and the other to keep track of the rocks around us. They were given an audio feed to listen too. This time it was Charna and Parmo, Tomer's parents, on watch.

"First off" dad said, "we could sit here and watch the drone feed, but that would take hours that we don't have. Valya, bring us up to date on the composite."

"Yes dear" as she adjusted the viewing screen built into the wall of the rec room. As the three dimensional image built up we could begin to see the unmistakable outlines of a ship of the Predecessors.

"I've had all of the drones data fed into a composer algorithm. As you can see from the resulting image the derelict is definitely one of the Predecessors." She waited for that to settle in. "Now I add in the asteroids around it" she touched a button on her keypad and more images appeared around the derelict.

Arson took over at this point. "I wasn't able to calculate many of their orbits" he started off, "but from what I was able to forecast, there is some gravitational attraction keeping them close around the hull. It's almost as if it was programmed to stay hidden."

"And what can we conclude from that?" Dad asked.

"I think that this ship is still alive. It may be abandoned, but I think it's waiting for someone to come back to it. We will have to approach it with extreme caution."

"Which to me" dad reasoned, "means that we will definitely need help." He looked at the faces around him. "Any comments or discussion?"

I sat in my seat unable to speak; I had found a derelict ship! I could hardly contain myself until I was rudely brought back to reality by Dora's slap to the back of my head. The look I gave her would have shriveled anyone else; but we're talking about Dora, she's impervious to me.

"Nice job, brother dear" she grudgingly whispered in my ear.

Slowly I smiled back at her. I tried to catch Arial's attention, but she was ignoring me, intent on what was going on between Dad and Arson.

Dad turned back to Arson. "Well captain, I abdicate to whatever you decide."

"Thanks Harkinson, I'll remember that." He thought

for a moment before addressing the rest of the crew. "I think we're operating in unknown territory here. Every artifact we've ever encountered of the Predecessors has been abandoned and empty, just discarded where it was. I don't believe that this derelict has been discarded. I believe that it was placed here to wait for them to come back. Why?" he shrugged. "There's no way to know."

"It is my opinion, and you can dispute it if you care too, that we should leave this one for the experts. So, should we send an Instagram? Let's look at it from every angle.

How much longer can we stay here before we have to refurbish? I know that it will be less than six months allowing for transport time back to base.

If we send for assistance, how long do you think it will take before we get a reply? Let's say it takes two weeks more or less before they reply. Then it will take how long before a ship can be readied and to get here. Probably another two years.

Let's face it, this derelict isn't going anywhere and the probability of someone else finding it is pretty small. We've got all we're going to get of visuals and we don't have the resources to handle the situation."

"So captain" dad replied dryly, "we pick up shop and head home taking all of our observations with us and we'll never get to see what we found?".

"That's my recommendation" he replied with a sigh.

"I'll say this though, if there's any way we can wrangle be-
coming part of the expedition, I'll do it."

"I wouldn't expect any less from you on that" dad
replied. "Probably wouldn't hurt to have a valid reason to
come back as well."

Dad turned to the rest of us. "Anyone else have any
feelings on this? Hearing none, then it's my recommendation that we finish up here and head back to base. Charna,
do either of you have any contacts on the artifacts council?"

Charna and Parma were the engineers; anything to
do with the ship was in their department. He was the big
blond haired type that didn't look like he knew how to tie
his shoes. But under that persistent grin was a heart of gold
and a mind like a steel trap. His wife Jarna, was a petite
blond. She almost looked like a pixie beside him, but was
also more outgoing and usually spoke for both of them.

"Harkinson, my man" her booming voice over the
intercom system, belied her size and demeanor, "there are
a couple of well-placed members on that board that owe
us quite a few favors." Then her voice brightened, "And I
think now is a good time to call them in. You can count on
us."

Then Charna's deep voice came over the intercom
voicing his opinion as well. "And the ship will be ready
when you are, captain."

"OK, last thing everyone, what's left to be done?"

Mom spoke up "I believe I can speak to that one

dear. There's nothing left of any more importance than heading back and getting the resources and help we need, then coming right back out here and get to work on our find!"

Dad looked at her strangely. "You really are up on this aren't you?"

"Yes Harkinson dear" as she smiled coquettishly at him.

"Then it's settled" dad sighed. "Let's make ready to head back."

CHAPTER 5

It was all hands working together to pull in all of the excavating machinery and stow it in the cargo hold.

"Jasom?" dad called.

"Yes sir." This sounded like business.

"Can I trust you to retrieve the satellite and then stow the flyer?"

"Yes sir" I replied brightly. Yeah, I get to do it instead of Arial. I quickly headed down to the hanger bay already in my suit. This was going to be the longest trip I had ever taken in the flyer and I was surprised that they were allowing me to do it. It was only a few hours trip inward to the third planet, and the satellite was easy enough to find. I slowly crept up to it and extended the arm to pull it in. After the arm stows it into the cargo hold I would have to disengage the arm and then manually go back into the hold to secure it in place.

As I was securing the satellite to its anchors in the cargo hold of the flyer, the alarm started screaming. It was going to have to wait, safety first, and that meant getting it tied into its harness properly. I tightened the last strap and slapped the hold cover back in place before crawling back up to the pilots chair to see what the alarm was all about.

A quick check showed it was a Queryl alert. There'd been a few of them lately but nothing close by, nothing so far to rate an alarm. There was a message attached which I read closely.

Jasom: We have received a strong indication that there are Queryl heading this way. Finish up stowing the satellite and hold a position off the planet's moon. Try to stay on the dark side and facing in our direction. I'll give you the all clear signal when they've passed by.

It was signed by Arson, Captain.

I did a quick check on supplies; I should be able to maintain position here for a few more days if it really came to that, longer if the base ship came closer to pick me up. I reviewed in my mind all of the procedures that we had for just these circumstances.

Unfortunately, Queryl were very unpredictable, but once they locked on to you the only chance was to run, that's why our ships had such strong propulsion units. There hasn't been a sign of any Queryl ever catching one of our ships, ever. Now a flyer, that's just like sitting in space with a sign out saying "Come and get me". As long as I kept the ship hidden from view I should be safe.

I used the smallest amount of propulsion to move the flyer into position on the dark side of the planets moon. The flyer could evade Earth's telescopes as long as it didn't get to close or move to fast. Earth's scientists hadn't developed high quality tracking devices yet.

With nothing but time on my hands I tapped into the local radio and television broadcasts. 1952 was an election year in the United States and I had learned many things about how the people of this country elected their leader. Oddly enough, a republican warrior was running against a democrat intellectual and appealing to the common people while his opponent was talking about how much good he could do.

Dad had told me about some of the political situations he had witnessed and it was usually the warrior that would come out ahead. This seemed to be the case as I listened to what they called polls where they asked people what they thought of each of the candidates and if they'd win the election or not. Dad had explained that the polls not only gave an insight into how the people thought but also influenced them as well.

"It is a classic example of the misuse of statistics!" He told me. "Applying statistical results from a large population onto a poll of people picked supposedly at random, but usually not, is like holding up a green card and telling everyone who cares to look at it, that it is a red card."

I listened, for lack of anything else to do. Some of it was interesting, watching both sides prattle on about how they were going to fix this and that and if they won the election all would be taken care of. Could a people be so stupid not to see that half of what they were being told just didn't make any sense? Glad I didn't live there.

"Squeawk! Bip, bip, bip, click" and then silence. That wasn't good, a tight beam compact message, short enough not to be traced easily. I stared at the console where a small red light blinked, awaiting my attention. I dreaded reading it.

Slowly I read the message all the way through for the third time. It was short and to the point.

Queryl onslaught imminent. Invoking emergency protocol Q-stat. Your orders are to proceed using protocol R-stat. Love Mom.

I stared at it again, how could they do this to me, their only son. I was pretty sure I knew what Q-stat was, but I brought it up on the console and read it all the way through. Essentially it was to run as fast as they could to Draconia-5, the nearest safe haven about twenty light years from here. If they could successfully lead them there, the safe haven had the resources to destroy the Queryl. Pretty much what I thought it would be, but what about me?

Then I read the R-stat protocol to which I will now

refer to as the Refugee Protocol. Dad and Captain Arson had agreed that it would not be possible to safely come and pick me up. Therefore, I was to land on this planet and blend in until they could come back and pick me up. Accounting for flight time in both directions plus hold over time at Draconia-5 it would be roughly about four years in Earth time before they could return.

Fear not son, we will do what we have to and be back here as soon as we can. I will send you an update as soon as we get to Draconia-5 and another when we leave so you will know when to expect us. Enclosed you will find valid documents to help you get settled in a place where we can find you. We will return for you.

Again I read through all of the documents before making any effort to proceed with their plan. For one thing it was hard to read the console through my bleary eyes, for another it was hard to get used to the feeling of being abandoned.

I slept fitfully for a few hours before deciding that the inevitable must be faced. Careful planning was required to be able to land unseen even in the decidedly rural area they had picked out. Reluctantly I plotted a course that would bring me in over the mountainous region of the northern United States, to the rolling eastern plains of one of the larger but sparsely populated states they called Montana.

The exact coordinates I had already programmed into the flight computer. The target was an abandoned farm on the outskirts of a small town called Nashua. Arson had tweaked with the land records office and purchased the farm in Dad's name. They already had planted records portraying the death of both of my parents after purchasing the property and that I was now the owner, albeit a minor. We were an immigrant family from some obscure country in Europe. It was also hinted that we were the royal family of that country as well. I'm not sure if royal was a good thing or not. Besides, at that point I didn't know the difference between a miner and a minor.

As darkness descended over the eastern Montana plains, the flyer dropped slowly through the planet's atmosphere. I had the receptors on full gain, if any detector beam locked on us...

"Ping, ping, ping!"

"What was that" I thought. Incoming object from behind, intercept two minutes, collision possible. I ran a quick analysis, nothing but a chunk of rock beginning its mad plunge into the planet's atmosphere where it would burn up long before reaching the ground. It would disintegrate probably about a hundred miles from where I was headed and at an altitude of several thousand feet.

I had an idea. Are there any others going my way? I could ride beside it and drop out from underneath it just before my target. I found a good candidate not far away already starting to slide down the gravity well, all I have to do is nudge it where I want it to go and hang in with it. It was considerably larger than the previous one and could possibly make it all the way to the ground. That would be better; watchers would be focused on it and might not notice my little tag along.

It took some wild calculations and more than a little luck to push it just a little here, once more over here, and then we're on our way.

I was feeling pretty proud of myself with coming up with this idea, all I had to do now was stay with it. That's when things didn't go quite as planned as my rock was leaving me behind.

I didn't count on the gravitational effect, I had instructed the flyer to take the slow approach. So much for instrument approach, I grabbed the controls and sped up to shadow my rock. The next thing I forgot about was the heat buildup from the friction between the rock and the atmosphere. The rock was glowing as the heat steadily built up, before long it would cease to exist. It wasn't until then that I noticed it was getting hotter in the flyer as well, time to slow down. I pared down the speed slowly as the rock gave off its last ounce of energy and vanished.

Time to target was down to minutes, I read off the data from the console and kept the course on visual with the target as its terminus. The console counted down to separation time, five, four, three, two, one…And I pulled sharply on the controls and swung the flyer around behind a low mountain and right into the field in front of the farm house. I scanned the fields and buildings for signs of life but there was nothing there but small animals.

I didn't have much time to get the flyer under cover, it should fit in the larger building with the big doors on the side, I believe it is called a barn. Not only was it the larger building, but it sat upon a rise with two large doors facing the other large building which was probably the house. It was dark outside the flyer, and I could just barely make out the outlines of the buildings. Dare I use the light? I decided not to and slowly climbed out of the flyer.

Just then there was a flash of light overhead followed by a rumbling noise off in the distance. I stood rooted to the spot not knowing what to do. Was there a war going on that we didn't know about? Then it happened again.

This time the flash of light was immediately followed by a loud bang and even louder rumbling followed by water falling out of the air. It sizzled when it hit the flyers hull which was still hot from the descent. I just happened to be looking in the right direction when the next flash came, a big long line of brilliant white light jumped from the ground into the clouds above and a rumbling so loud it made my teeth chatter.

I was witnessing a normal weather phenomenon of the planet called lightening; the rumbling noise was caused by the thousands of joules of energy flashing through the

air causing an audible heat wave. The water was called…
rain, that's what it is. I climbed back into the flyer, my
clothes were all wet and I was getting cold.

"I'll have to spend the night in the flyer" I thought.
"Hopefully no one will be prowling around out here in this
weather." I rummaged around in the cargo hold in the back
and found a coverall. It must have belonged to Arson, the
sleeves and legs were a little long, but it was all I could find
and they were dry.

The rain stopped a few hours later and the clouds
gave way to a clear sky dominated by a large bright moon.
I hopped out of the flyer and ran over to the barn. The two
big doors looked sturdy enough and I quickly slid them
open. It would be a tight fit, but the opening inside was
large enough to hold the flyer. In the waning light of the
moon, I managed to back it into an enclosed area in the
further end of the barn. It was dusty in there and there was
all sorts of decaying vegetable growths lying everywhere.
I had provisions enough to get by for several more days
which meant that I should start looking for food as soon
as I could. But for now, I needed more rest. I closed the
barn doors and climbed back into the flyer and went back
to sleep.

CHAPTER 6

As I opened my bleary eyes the next morning, I slowly remembered where I was and how things had come about to put me here. I was essentially abandoned on a foreign planet with limited knowledge on how to survive.

Outside the flyers windows I could see sunlight streaming through the windows of the barn, and there was dust everywhere. Even the flyer had dust caked on it; it had been wet when I moved it into the barn.

I checked the console on the outside conditions, temperature, humidity, air content and pressure, all within safe limits. Slowly I read again the R-stat procedure that Arson had sent me. Somehow it didn't reassure me very much. What do I do first? Then it occurred to me that I had already done what was required first, land on the planet. What do I do next? Blend in, the procedure says.

"Well, it ain't going to happen if I stay in here" I thought, mimicking some of the slang I had heard on one of the broadcasts Dora had forced me to listen too. Maybe they had been useful after all.

I climbed out of the flyer and decided to explore the barn. It was dusty inside and the smells were very strange. There was a large open space above the flyer which wrapped around both sides leaving the center area open all the way to the roof. There were a couple of rooms off the main area containing all sorts of strange items. The next door disclosed a set of stairs going down into the lower level. The opening was nearly clogged with hairy fibers that hung everywhere in the stairway. I grabbed a loose stick and waved it in the opening gathering the wispy stuff up as I descended the staircase. The gray fibrous stuff was hanging everywhere.

Down below, the floor underneath was a hard rough gray stone like substance with cracks here and there and troughs in other places. Metal piping ran from floor to ceiling in a long row with a trough in the floor several feet behind it and a three foot walkway beyond that to the outer wall. Evenly spaced windows let some light into the darkened space. On the wall to my right was a dusty white box with a switch on it. I flipped the switch but nothing seemed to happen. With nothing more to look at, I went back up the stairs and over to the barn doors. Inset in the left hand door was a smaller door with a simple latch.

The mechanical operation was simple, grab the handle and my thumb rested on a flat plate. When I squeezed, it unhooked the latch and the door swung open.

I swung the door open and close a few times watching how the latch worked. I stepped through the door and walked up to the house.

The house was approximately fifty to sixty feet on a side and two levels high with a wedge shaped top on it. There were several windows, on each level of each side and a sort of platform with a roof over it on the side facing toward the valley. There was a large door flanked with a vertical row of little windows on each side in the middle of that wall of the house. There was another door on the side of the house facing the barn. I kept looking for signs of people as I approached the side door. Again, the latch was simple and the door wasn't locked.

On the first level the side door let into a large room with a table surrounded by several chairs, possibly an eating area; most of the rest of what was in that room would take time to understand. A corridor led down the center of the house toward the end with the big door. Just inside the big door was a set of stairs that went up to the upper level.

On each side was a large room, each having a set of doors with glass panes. The smaller of the two rooms had more ornate furniture and looked less used; probably for formal occasions where the other room was for ordinary uses. I climbed the stairs.

At the top of the stairs a corridor ran all the way to the back of the house with two or three doors on each side. Looking inside I could see that all but one of them were for sleeping. The rooms toward the front were larger with a single large bed and the rooms toward the rear had single or bunk beds. The extra room was only about ten feet square but its functions were not readily apparent. There were several different white fixtures with piping attached.

At the back end of the corridor were two more doors, the first had another set of stairs going up into the roof area. Using my flashlight I quickly took a look around from the top of the stairs, but all I could see was just stuff stored anywhere it would fit; everything in sight was covered in dust. I would have to leave this for some time in the future. I closed that door and opened the other one.

Now this was something different, I stepped through the door onto a rough surface in a completely empty space with slanting ceilings. The only light, besides the flashlight I'd brought with me, came from a single window looking toward the barn. I slowly walked further on until I came to a set of stairs that led down to another door. This was a single large room about the same floor size as the room above. There were only a couple of windows with a door between. Against the rear wall there was a bed, some odd shelving, and a cabinet with piping in the corner. There was another door that let into an area under the stairway I had just come down. Inside the door was a very small room with a low shelf with two oval holes in it. The rest of the space was empty, and like everything else in this part of the house, covered in a thick layer of dust. No one had been in here in a long time by the looks of it.

I stepped out of the door into the morning light. The house had been painted a bright white trimmed with a dark green, most of which was now peeling. The part I had just come from was a dark brownish black in color, and no sign that it had ever been painted at all.

There were no indications from the stories I'd watched with Dora that would explain what I had just seen. I would probably never understand what the reasons were anyway nor do I think I should waste my time trying to figure it out; I would only be here for a few years at most.

I went back into the eating area. Beside the corridor that ran to the front of the house was another door. It contained another set of stairs that went down into an underground area. I couldn't remember the name for it, but it would take months to figure out what some of the things stored down there were. I shone my flashlight around in the gloom; there were more of those gray wispy fibers hanging down here too.

In back of the stairs was an area with several rows of floor to ceiling shelving. I would guess that some of the glass jars on the shelves may have been edible but I put that off for another time.

Two days later I had successfully tested several of the jars in the underground room. They were edible and extremely tasty, some sort of a sweet fruit, but not sufficient for a complete diet. I have managed to catch some of the smaller animals and once cooked over a small fire they aren't too bad, just have to smother them in the sap from one of the jars. There are enough jars to go for several more days and if I can catch enough small animals I should be able to survive.

I have also made a complete survey of the entire household and discovered running water in the small room on the upper level that I've come to understand are the toilet and bathing facilities; there is also a smaller version beside the cooking room. The chairs in the front rooms are quite comfortable and the wider bench size chairs are big enough to sleep on. There are blankets in a small room at the top of the stairs and closets of clothes in one of the larger sleeping rooms. Some of the fastenings were a little strange, but I found some that fit fairly well.

It was lonely out here, but I was beginning to get used to it. Each morning and evening I would go out to the flyer to check for messages; so far I have been disappointed. It was going to be a long few years.

I had also started monitoring the local radio broadcasts trying to find out more about where I was. I knew that I was in the town of Nashua, but it didn't have a radio station, the only one in the area was from a place called Williston in North Dakota. I found another one closer by while listening at night, but it was a small station that didn't have enough power to reach very far in this hilly area and all they played was this strange music that made me depressed just listening to it. Something like Hank Williams, I think that was what they called it.

I had spent some time exploring the contents of the underground room, it was larger than I first thought. There were many jars whose contents varied in color from bright greens to oranges, reds, and several shades in between. Down on the bottom shelves were some large containers, some with a flat top, the others had a narrow top with a plug. I haven't found a way to pull a plug to see what is inside them yet, maybe later.

On one of the top shelves, down near the end, were several more jars that contained a clear liquid. The first one was only half full so I pulled it down and snapped the latch that held the cover on. First you smell it, so I took a deep breath and inhaled. I almost threw the jar as my eyes started tearing up from the smell. Whatever could this stuff be? It smelled like high octane fuel. It might be highly explosive so I carefully put the cover back on and put it back on the shelf. Someday I might just find a use for that stuff I thought. But why would they store it with the food though? Another mystery.

CHAPTER 7

So I now know that today is Thursday the 5th day of June in the year of 1952. I had taken to marking down the days and learning about the calendar, a strange conglomeration of 12 months having either 30 or 31 days except for February which can have either 28 or 29 depending on if the year is evenly divisible by four. Not only that, but people don't work on the days that begin with the letter S. But barbers don't work on Mondays and do on Saturdays. Nobody works on Sundays but farmers still have to feed and care of their animals, even on Sundays. Very confusing these people are.

I shook my head again, closed the flyer up, and made my way back to the house.

I didn't notice the automobile sitting at the foot of the driveway until I heard someone call me.

"Well hey there son, we've been a lookin' for yah." I almost tripped over my feet turning around to see who was there.

There were two people standing there, the man who spoke was taller than I am, dressed in a brown suit with a dirty green tie. The other was a woman, also dressed in brown and wearing a small black hat with some sort of netting on it. She only smiled while he did all of the talking.

"You are Jason Kingston aren't you?" he asked. His smile seemed frozen in place.

I stumbled over the question thinking furiously what to say. We'd learned the language, and Dora had insisted on speaking in it as well, but I knew we weren't pronouncing it properly. I'd try the safe way.

"Uh, Yes sir" with just a little quaver to my voice.

"Good, good. First our condolences on the loss of your family" he was looking around at the buildings. "Have you been living here all by yourself?"

"Uh, yes sir." This wasn't going very well; it didn't look like they were going to leave any time soon.

"Mr. Dressler, we should introduce ourselves" the woman said. "I'm sure he has no idea who we are and why we're here."

"You're right as usual, Mrs. Martin" and he turned back to me. "Son, my name is Herbert Dressler and I'm the county truancy officer. This here is Mrs. Martin and she's the school superintendent for the county." He searched my face for any signs of recognition. "You don't know what that means do you?"

"Uh, no sir." Things were definitely not going well at all, how was I going to get out of this? Could he catch me before I got into the barn? If I could make it to the flyer I'd be out of here.

"You ain't thinking of runnin' are you son? I was the fastest runner in high school, you won't get far. If you run it will go harder on yah. Best you come along quietly, Yah hear?"

I looked at the woman's face, it was completely passive. If he was as fast as he thought he was I didn't have a chance of getting to the flyer. Best not to let him know it was there either, that would be too much to explain.

"What's truancy mean sir?" I ventured.

"Heh, heh, it means I get to go find all the kids that aren't in school and punish them." He even looked like he enjoyed it too.

"Why punish them?"

"You ain't from around here are you?" He seemed a little unsure of how to handle me.

I'll have to tread a fine line here, keep him guessing but don't push him too far. I managed to keep an innocent look on my face. "Our family just emigrated here from Europe; I'm not familiar with anything.

"And he has lost all of his family Mr. Dressler. That means he's an orphan, lost and all alone." She smiled at me again. "And I think I know just how to help him out."

"Now Mrs. Martin" he replied patronizing her, "I'll

just take him over to the jail and hold him until we get everything straightened out."

"Not this time" she replied firmly. "I remember what happened to the Colliers little girl that you carted off like that. The county might not take well to finding out what really happened to her do you think?"

Before he could reply she walked over and took my hand. "Come with me Jason, I know exactly what to do with you." and we walked down behind Mr. Dressler's car to her car which I hadn't noticed before. It was a bright red color with shiny chrome accents. We waited until Mr. Dressler had gotten into his car and left before she turned to me.

"How long have you been out here all alone?"

"I don't know exactly, been sort of hanging around." It was a lame answer, but I hoped it encouraged a little empathy on her part. Of the alternatives I would rather go with what she had in mind than what Mr. Dressler had in mind. I might have had to hurt him if things got out of hand.

"And your whole family is gone?"

I wasn't sure what she was fishing for, maybe I should tell her a few more things.

"Yeah, they've all gone, the whole place is in my name now. But I don't know what to do with it."

"OK, how old are you Jason Kingston?'

"Well let's see here" I did some quick mental arithmetic, "I guess about 15." I knew she was going to ask what day and month, I'll have to pick those as well.

"Just one more question then, what year are you in school?"

"That I really don't know, they use a different system back in Europe." That might have been a lie, but I really didn't know so I'll call it an imaginative guess.

"True enough" she replied thoughtfully. "How would you like to live with a family I know in town? They don't have any children of their own and I'm sure they would be delighted to take you in."

"Why can't I just live here?" I really needed to stay near the flyer.

"I don't think you have much choice in the matter, truancy means you have to attend school. Or would you rather have Mr. Dressler take you in?" She gave me a look that made a shiver run up my spine. "Those are your only choices" she replied dryly.

CHAPTER 8

Ned and Henrietta Johnson were nice enough I guess, he ran the general store in town and they lived upstairs. They could sense the misgivings I had about the arrangements, but I was left with no alternative.

"Mrs. Martin said you were from Europe?" Mr. Johnson asked. "What happened to the rest of your family?"

Before I could come up with an answer, Mrs. Johnson came to my rescue.

"Nedwick!" she scolded, "Where is your compassion? The boy has lost all of his family and needs a place to live."

"Now Henrietta" he replied, "I'm just trying to find out where he's from."

I could tell from his voice that he was used to losing these arguments. That was a good thing for me, all I had to do was play on her sentiments and he'd be no problem.

I decided to risk it and told them all that had been

in the R-stat folder that Arson had sent me. In the process he had included a complete background for me including birthday and place. I had only remembered the year.

Henrietta Johnson was a stocky woman, I guess that's the right term, and very strong minded. She told me that she grew up on a small farm in South Dakota. Ned, as everyone else called him, grew up down in Billings. They had met at the USO club, whatever that was, in Billings just as he was being shipped out to Hawaii right after the war started. They started writing and when he came back from the war she was waiting for him.

He had been in the Army, a supply division. By the end of the war he'd had several promotions and accumulated a good amount of knowledge in how to run a store. They were married and bought the store here in Nashua the very next year.

They were childless as Ned had contracted mumps as a child and it left him unable to father children. They had thought about adoption, but being way out in the middle of nowhere didn't help that cause any. So now I was to be their foster child. After a few days I began to see the advantages of the situation, steady meals and a comfortable place to live.

Mrs. Martin stopped in on Friday to see if I was settled and told me that I would have to take some placement tests. They needed to see what grade to put me in and the summer months would be perfect for any remedial work I'd have to do. It also made little sense to put me into what was left of the present school year as there were only a couple of days left anyway.

Mrs. Johnson took me over to the superintendent's office later that afternoon and one of the assistants in the office took me into an inner office and handed me a packet and a pencil.

"You have 30 minutes to finish" she said. "When I signal the end you will put down the pencil and I will collect the packet; any questions?" Before I could ask, she put the packet on the desk in front of me and sat down in a corner chair and started reading a book.

Inside the packet were several pages and an answer sheet. I puzzled out that each numbered question on the sheet had multiple lettered answers. The answer sheet had a number and an empty box beside it. That seemed simple enough.

The questions were hard as I had no idea what they were asking and each answer looked just like the other with just a slight difference. I had to resort to guessing again.

The last page was on math. I knew most of the symbols, enough to make better guesses I thought. But it still took time to convert from the symbols I was use to into what they used here. At the end of the thirty minutes I was mentally fried and the sweat was pouring down my face. The timer dinged and the woman closed her book and came over and picked up my packet.

"Just leave the pencil on the desk and wait in the outer office while I check your answers" as she herded me out the door.

I sat in a chair by the front door collecting my thoughts. This was going to be one of the hardest things I had ever done, trying to blend in with a culture that has nearly nothing in common with what I'm familiar with.

"Are they done with you yet Jason?" Mrs. Johnson asked as she poked her head in the door. One look at me and she put her hand over her mouth. "Oh dear me, this will never do. You just wait right here Jason, let me find out what's going on."

By the look on her face something very interesting was about to happen.

"Rachel!" She yelled. "Get your sloppy butt out here right now.

The woman assistant that had given me the test jumped up from where she was lamely talking on the phone. The shocked look on her face made me chuckle inside but I kept my face impassive.

"Yes ma'am? What can I do for you?" as she slowly walked over to the front counter that was all that stood between her and Mrs. Johnson.

"Have you checked the results of his test yet?" She wasn't letting up a bit.

"Ah, no ma'am, Mrs. Martin is the only one with the key. I'll have to wait for her to do it. She's in a meeting at the moment; can I have her call you?" There was still a slight quaver to her voice.

"Rachel, you have less than one minute to get her out here before I really start getting mean."

Rachel just stood there not knowing what to do.

"Rachel?" Mrs. Johnson was starting to get real mad.

"Yes ma'am?" I could just imagine her knees shaking.

Mrs. Johnson leaned on the counter, "Do it now!" she whispered menacingly.

Rachel's face turned a little pale, "Yes ma'am" was all she said before scurrying down the hallway at the back of the office and out of sight.

"Stupid woman thinks she's so high and mighty, one of these days she's going to goof off to much and there'll be hell to pay." Mrs. Johnson muttered, before turning to me. "Don't think that means that you can talk that way to her. You hear me?"

Now I knew how Rachel felt, "No ma'am."

She stared at me as if she could see right into my inner thoughts, this woman was really scary. Just then Mrs. Martin came out from the back and walked calmly up to the counter. "Henrietta, so nice to see you again." She spoke soothingly.

"Skip the pleasantries Judith, how'd our little Martian boy do on his placement tests?" Still sounding a little irritated.

"Why don't we go back to my office and we'll just look them over together." She opened the little door and let Mrs. Johnson through. "And that goes for you too Jason" she continued musically.

I quickly hustled through and followed them to another much larger office further along the back hallway from where I took the test.

I sat in a corner of the office as Mrs. Martin went over the test results. I could see the puzzled expressions on her face and knew I was in for trouble.

"Henrietta, would you mind waiting out in the office while I go over these with Jason? I promise it won't be long and then I'll talk to you about what he'll have to do from there."

After Mrs. Johnson left Mrs. Martin took a long look at me and shook her head. "I'm not sure what to make of these results other than to throw them away." She pondered for a moment before continuing. "Let me think about this, these tests are designed for someone who has a modest understanding of things as they are. You're not from around here so things like geography and basic American culture would have no relevance to you." She gave me another stern look. "You understand the consequences here don't you?"

I nodded that I did.

"I thought as much, and considering the way you talk I can see that you possess a certain amount of education." Not seeing any response "So let's try it this way."

For the next twenty minutes she went back over every question in the test, made sure I understood what it asked and then we went over the answers making sure that I was the one who made the choice. She noted my choice and we moved on to the next one.

By explaining each question I could see how the test was structured. I made the comment that by making the answers so close in meaning it added a level of confusion making the results less valid. That comment got me a strange look from her.

Next we went over the math questions and with the help of paper diagrams I explained the answer and how I derived it. I also made the comment that on three of the questions none of the answers were correct. Math is a tool, a process by which you apply all of the variables in the proper order, using the necessary functions, and the correct answer is the result.

She was very shocked by my comment and when we finished going over all of the questions on the test she put it all back in the packet, including all of my diagrams.

"I need to speak with Henrietta now, send her back and you can wait for us out front. And try to stay out of trouble." She thought a moment then "best you don't speak unless spoken to and say as little as possible when you do. Understood?"

"Yes, play dumb." And I smiled at her.

"We'll make an American out of you yet" as she smiled in return.

I sat in the outer office for most of an hour before they came back out. Mrs. Johnson looked a little disturbed, but Mrs. Martin looked like she was facing a big challenge.

"Jason, I'll expect to see you back here again on Monday morning about nine o'clock. We'll go over what subjects you will be studying during the summer. Henrietta, if you have any further questions please let me know."

Mrs. Johnson didn't have much to say all the way back to the store. She parked the car in the garage out back and we went up the back stairs. It was getting late in the afternoon so she went right into the kitchen and started making supper. This was one of the biggest advantages to living here, she was an excellent cook. Not knowing what to do I watched her as she prepared the food, adding this to that all the while tasting the result. I also closely watched how the appliances worked.

"Mrs. Johnson?"

"That's going to have to change" she replied sternly as she stirred the stew on the stove. "I think you should call us Henrietta and Nedwick." She glanced back over her shoulder. "How would that be? After all, you're going to be living with us now."

"Uh, that would be fine...Henrietta?"

"I think you'll get used to it. You're a smart boy Jason, Judith said so, probably smarter than most anyone in town, I'd say."

I denoted a sense of pride in that statement. "Just what did the test results say?" I asked her.

"It was not so much what they said; I think you impressed her with your math and verbal skills. We agreed that the tests were not even close to determining what grade to place you in. She's going to tailor a study plan that you can do at home. Nedwick and I will help you with it. It's more to acquaint you with what we all take for granted and maybe we'll all learn a few things from you as well."

I hoped she didn't misinterpret the shocked feeling I had at that last part. I had to keep to the designs in the R-stat.

"I'll still need to go out to my farm to check on things."

"You won't have to worry too much about that, the place hasn't been vacant all that long. I'll get Nedwick's brother to go out and lock it up and turn the water off and such."

"But there's some stuff out there that I need, personal stuff."

"Just tell him where it is and he can pick it up for you" as she tested the stew.

"I hid it and I'd rather not tell anyone where my hiding place is." I hope that wasn't too much of an attitude.

"Well, I suppose you could ride out with him..." Then she gave me a smirk. "You think he'll get into the moonshine don't you?" She thought a little bit on that. "Yes, I think it's best I come along as well. You know where it's kept don't you?" I managed a shy nod. "Thought as much, there is more to you than meets the eye isn't there?" as she went back to making supper. I wonder what moonshine is.

She glanced at the clock above the stove. "Almost five, why don't you go down and help Nedwick close up the store. When you get back I'll show you how to set the table."

CHAPTER 9

I headed down the inside staircase that led into the back office. The doors were kept locked to prevent anyone from sneaking up the back stairs. Out front Nedwick was just locking the door and turning the sign around.

He nodded to me. "Just about done down here, soon as you get your studies set up we'll start getting you into working down here. Keep you out of Henrietta's hair. Do that too often and she might just bite your head off" he chuckled. "How'd the testing go?"

"I thought it was a mess, didn't understand half of it" I replied sullenly. I wasn't sure if he was going to punish me for failing it.

"Don't put much faith in them anyway" he remarked calmly, "just a bunch of mumbo jumbo. Who was giving you the test?" I told him. "Hah! That useless twig? She wouldn't know which end of a horse was pointed north."

"She doesn't know how to use a compass?" I asked

remembering how Henrietta had talked to her.

He laughed out loud at that. "Oh my, you better watch what you say Jason, you're bound to stomp on some toes. Let's head up to supper."

I was really beginning to understand my good fortune in being placed in the Johnson's care, they were really nice people.

The rest of the evening went by rather well. It took some getting used to calling them by Henrietta and Nedwick. And then he insisted that I call him just Ned. Strangely Henrietta seemed happy about that. I had a lot to learn; especially in dealing with people.

The next day was Saturday and Ned wanted me to learn some things about the store. We went down early in the morning before the store opened and he showed me where the stock was kept, why each particular item was stored where it was, and that it would be my job to help unload the trucks when they came in and to help the customers with their purchases.

"When you get a little further along in your studies I'll teach you how the accounting system works and how to do the pricing. How familiar are you with our currency?"

He studied my face for a moment. "From the shocked look on your face I'll take that as a no. Before you can really get along around here you have to know how the currency works. I was stationed in several different countries when I was in the war. Each time I learned the currency before the language. Remember this, Money talks!"

From the confused look on my face he tried a different angle. "Say you wanted that box over there. How much does it cost?"

I went over and picked up the box. It said Paper clips quantity 100 with a small circular figure and the number 15 stamped on the top. I still looked confused.

"OK" he said, "bad example. What I was trying to say is, if you have money you're more likely to get what you want with only a slim understanding of the language."

The store was only open for a few hours on Saturday morning so people could pick up things they'd need before Monday. I used the time to stroll through the aisles taking inventory of where everything was placed.

"Jason?" Ned called from the front where he was talking with a woman that had just come in. "Do you know where the Olive Oil is? Could you bring up a jar for Mrs. Wright, please?"

As it turned out I was standing right beside it. I picked up the bottle and carried it up to the front and set it on the counter. "Anything else, Mrs. Wright" I asked.

She stared at me in shock for a moment as if to ask who I was. "Oh yes, you're that Jason boy got left out at the old Barton farm. Is he working for you Mr. Johnson?"

"No Mrs. Wright" he replied jovially, "he's our foster son" he replied putting his arm around me. "Aren't you son?"

"Yes sir…I mean yes Ned" as I smiled at her also.

"Why how nice" she said beaming at both of us, "you know, I think I'll get a couple of other things since I'm already here."

I guess we made a good impression on her. I helped her carry her bags out to her truck and set them behind the seat; she waved at me as she drove away. By then it was noon and Ned closed up the store and we climbed the back stairs to see what Henrietta was up too.

When we got to the kitchen there was a basket setting on the table.

"Well I'll be" he said brightly, "looks like someone wants to go on a picnic" Ned laughed. He looked at my blank face, "don't worry Jason, it'll be fun. Grab your jacket it might get a little chilly later on."

CHAPTER 10

A half hour later we pulled into the driveway of my farm. It didn't look like anything had been disturbed. The sun was shining down on the front porch and there were little insects flying everywhere as we spread a blanket on the ground in front of the house.

"You can set on the porch any time you want, but it's more fun to set on the ground" Henrietta chided me when I looked aghast at her spreading the blanket on the grass in front of the house. "Why don't you roam around and make sure everything is where it should be and I'll get things put together here. Ned, would you give me a hand."

I roamed around the back side of the house and slipped down behind the barn without being seen and slipped in the lower entrance to the barn and up the stairs. I knew what I had to do and didn't have much time to do it in.

I slipped into the flyer and checked for messages. Nothing yet, but it had only been ten days so far, it would be several weeks before I could expect to hear from them. I had to completely conceal the flyer before anyone spotted it. I grabbed the R-stat printout and stuffed it in my pocket and started covering the front of the flyer with some boards I had found in one of the rooms then covered it all with the stuff people called hay. When I was done the flyer was completely concealed. To be safe I fixed the doors so they couldn't open from the outside and climbed out one of the side windows.

I stole back around the side of the barn to the back side of the house where the empty rooms were. Then I went up the back staircase and into the second level of the house. I needed to use the bathroom and when I flushed the toilet and stepped back into the hallway Ned was standing there.

"Henrietta's waiting for us, you head on down, I've got to use the facilities." With that he went into the bathroom and closed the door.

I stood in the hallway a moment before heading down the front staircase and out the front door to sit on the steps.

"Now where did Nedwick go too?"

"He said he had to use the facilities. There's another smaller one down by the kitchen if you need one." From the look on her face I must have said something wrong. Then it passed.

"You have a nice place here, how have you managed to survive?" she asked.

"By stuff in jars underneath the house and small animals I could catch." She gave me a disgusted look. "But they weren't very tasty" I hastily added. "Your cooking is very much better."

"All things considered that's not saying very much." She saw the look on my face. "Now, now, Jason; what I meant to say is that those types of small animals are not considered good to eat. Oh why are we talking about this anyway? Ned!" she hollered, "Where are you?"

I'd heard the toilet flush quite a while back. "I think I know where he is." I guided her down the stairs and into the room with all of the shelves.

I heard her say "Oh my." when she saw all the jars neatly lined up on the shelves. When we got back to the last row where what I thought was fuel was stored we found Ned. He had the cover off the half full jar and was just sniffing it.

"You're not going to try drinking that are you?" she asked, "last I checked that stuff would melt the finish off a cars bumper."

He looked a little sheepish. "I'd heard that old man Barton had quite a still hidden up in the hills. After looking around down here, I think the still was right here in the cellar. "I bet this stuff has really aged well" as he looked lovingly at the half full jar.

"Times like this I don't know you Nedwick." She looked at me. "How much of this stuff have you found?"

"I've been through the whole cellar" tasting the new word I had just learned, "and this is all I've found. I wouldn't doubt that there are other hiding places as well."

"The still is stored in that room over there" Ned admitted, "the door with all the cobwebs on it, hasn't been touched in a couple of years or more. Any of it hidden in the barn?" he asked me.

"Don't think so, been completely through it as well. Only place I haven't really explored much is the back side of the house. It's completely empty but there might be some hiding places in there as well." I pointed to the unpainted addition on the back side of the house.

"Ah, the servant's quarters." He looked at Henrietta.

"Food will wait a little longer" she said, "and I'm coming along just to make sure you two don't get into any more trouble."

After going through the servants quarters, from the outhouse under the stairs, all the way up through the upper level and on into the bedrooms on the upper level we checked for hidden panels or loose floorboards. The only stash, as Ned called it, was in the cellar.

"You know it wouldn't be a good thing to leave all of this stuff here in the cellar." Ned said. "We should pack it all in the car and take it home with us. After all" he said, "It actually belongs to Jason and we are his guardians."

Henrietta glared at him thinking only of the jar he

still held in his hand.

"And that includes all of the preserves as well. We should eat well next winter."

I could see that the part about the preserves really appealed to her. "What's in the containers underneath?" I asked.

They looked where I was pointing. Henrietta said something I didn't understand under her breath, Ned's face lit up and his jaw just dropped open. This must be something very important.

"The crocks, the ones with the wooden lids contain brine stock and other types of preserved food stuffs." She told me.

"And the ones with the small tops?" I prompted.

"Each one of those jugs contains about eight gallons" Ned gulped, "and each of these here jars holds a pint, and there are eight pints in a gallon." Ned commented as he looked down each of the rows beneath the shelves. "There are ten jugs under each row of shelves, and six rows of shelves."

"Stop drooling Nedwick! How much money does that work out to be?"

"I'll make it easy, at a dollar a pint jar, that works out to almost four thousand dollars."

This time Henrietta's mouth dropped open. "Lordy, Lordy, what in the world are we going to do with all of it?"

"Why not just leave it where it is?" I asked.

"Because if anyone gets a hint at what's down here, there's going to be one hell of a fight over it." Henrietta murmured.

"What is the stuff good for anyway? I thought from the smell that it was some sort of fuel." I still felt queasy thinking that Ned was actually going to drink it.

"I ain't having any of this stuff anywhere near our place. I say we bury it right here and now" she exclaimed.

Ned looked horrified at that. "We can't do that! That would be…" He ran out of words as she glared back at him.

"How about a compromise?" I asked.

I made them a compromise that seemed to satisfy. I told them I had a place where nobody would ever find it, but I would have to be the only one that knew where it was. Ned balked a little at first, but Henrietta nudged him a little and he gave in.

She told him the only other alternative was to dump it all down the drain. Ned sadly gave in and asked if he could help. That was the fatal flaw in my plan, the crocks were too heavy to carry; there was no way to get them out of the cellar. On to the backup plan.

It took some cajoling to get Henrietta to agree, but we settled on moving them into the back room of the cellar, stashing them behind the clutter that Ned said was the still. As we were moving the crocks into the dark inside corner hidden behind the door he explained all about what the terms "Moonshine", "White Lightening", "Hooch", and

"Sourmash" meant and how certain people were so good at it that it looked just like water and had very little smell.

"Ned, if it's not supposed to smell, then this stuff is nothing but fuel, it smells really bad. You may be able to burn it in your automobile."

"Not so my boy, that first jug contains Kerosene to discourage anyone from drinking any of it. Here, I opened the last one on the shelf just to make sure."

I took a whiff out of the completely full jar. I couldn't quite place the smell. "What is this stuff anyway?"

"That's the best dang illegal alcohol I've ever seen." We were all alone down there. "Here, take a sip." He let me take a little sip. Then he laughed at the expression on my face. He quickly closed the lid and set the jar aside.

When I could breathe again, and my eyes cleared up, I just gave him a weird look. "People actually drink this stuff? Why?" He just laughed at me.

"What are you two delinquents up to down there?" Henrietta hollered down the stairs, she was getting impatient.

"Just finished dear" Ned hollered back up.

"Well hurry up, we still have to load up the preserves we're taking back with us."

Henrietta just couldn't resist taking some of the jars containing fruits and vegetables. She did ask me if it was alright since, by rights, they essentially belonged to me, as did all of the Hooch. I liked that name the best.

Ned closed and locked the door and we climbed back upstairs. He helped me lock all the windows and doors on the house then we loaded about twenty jars of food stuffs in the trunk of the car.

"Jason, do you plan on keeping the farm?" Ned asked. "You know you can live with us as long as you want."

"Ah, I've kind of grown attached to it, I want to keep it. Do you want me to sell it?"

"Not so much that son, but the taxes are coming due and if they aren't paid the town will sell it off."

"What are taxes?" I know it sounded lame, but I hadn't a clue what he was referring too.

"The town collects taxes from everyone in town that owns property based on its value. That money goes for town upkeep, pays the town employees to plow the roads in the winter, those sorts of things. How much land is there besides the buildings?"

I told him what I knew about it. "I have the papers that I was given but haven't really looked at them that much."

"Dig them out and when we get home we'll figure something out."

After supper we sat around the kitchen table and went over the papers that Arson had left me. He showed me what all the descriptions meant and where the property values were located. It also said that I owed $150 in taxes for the coming quarter.

"I don't have $150" I told Ned, "Does that mean I'm going to lose the farm?"

"You have a couple of choices, but first let's take a look at all of the land that you own. Too bad we couldn't just sell…"

"Nedwick Johnson! I'll hear none of that." Henrietta roared.

With a red face Ned continued. "One option is to sell off a small parcel of land, but let's see what's growing first."

The next day he and I went back to the farm and walked as much of the fields as we could. The last field we walked through had a high growing grass in it Ned said that was wheat. The one across the road had corn. I memorized what the plants looked like and we marked those on a paper that matched which field they were in.

"Amazing luck there Jason, you've got well over forty acres of corn and nearly a hundred of wheat. Mr. Barton probably used some of the corn to make his hooch with and sold the rest. Let me ask around, what we may be able to do is sell the standing grains to some of the other local farmers in the fall and still have a bit left over. There's still quite a bit of the growing season left, but I'll check around and see what we can do."

Later on that summer at harvest time, all of the corn and wheat were spoken for and most of the fields of grass had already had an early cutting. I made significantly more than the taxes and Ned helped me open a bank account to put it in.

CHAPTER 11

Monday morning and I was back in the superintendent's office with Mrs. Martin. There was also another man standing there dressed in a black suit with a red bow tie. I had been reading some of the magazines that the Johnson's kept in their living room. It was a big help in learning some of the more social things in life.

"Good morning Jason, I'd like you to meet Mr. Sanders, he's from the state supervisory board."

I looked him over as he was doing the same of me. He was wearing round glasses with thin wire frames and I don't think he ever smiled.

"What is your full name young man?" he asked.

"Jasom Gregory Kingston, sir" I replied quickly recalling what Arson had setup in the R-stat.

"Is it Jasom or Jason?"

"It is Jasom sir, most people just say Jason but it really is spelled with an m." I kept my voice impassive just to see what his intentions were.

"Mrs. Martin tells me that the test you were given has flaws in it, you know anything about that?" Still with the same dry tone of voice.

A quick glance at Mrs. Martin led me to believe that I should play it dumb.

"Well, some of the questions asked about things I've never heard of, I didn't grow up around here or go to school in this country. Many of those things aren't taught where I came from." That should be enough.

"Fair enough, I suppose. What do you expect to get out of this summer study program then?"

"Hopefully, enough to be able to fit in" I replied without elaboration.

"Mrs. Martin?"

She didn't respond at first, her attention was focused on something going on in the back of the office area. "Oh! Yes, Mr. Sanders?"

"You have interviewed him quite extensively I understand. Do you think that this course of study will have him ready in time for school this fall?" He intoned dryly.

"Yes Mr. Sanders, he should fit in quite well in most areas" she replied.

For some reason I was missing something here, these two were talking like perfect strangers but I was sure they knew each other quite well. It felt like this was all just an act.

"I sense you have some misgivings" he looked annoyed.

"Social skills will be a problem, he is only marginal in conversational language, but I fear that we may be holding him back in math and science."

There were a few other things she wasn't telling him either.

"So you will be placing him based on the social limitations?"

"Mr. Sanders, I don't want to hold him back from what he is capable of doing, but to put him in with a class that doesn't challenge him we could lose him entirely."

"All right" he said, turning his attention to me, "what do you think about all of this?"

He gazed at me searching for any signs of rebellion I guess, but I kept an impassive face.

"Judith, I think I agree with your assessment, behind that quiet exterior is a very interesting person with some very big secrets." He said the last with a smile on his face. "You also know how to control your temper and you're going to have to rely on your better judgment in the coming school year." He put out his hand and I took it. "You ever have any problems, just call on me or Mrs. Martin here, and we'll do what we can to help you out. Good luck son and study hard. I will be watching your progress closely."

It would be several years later before I would come to realize just how closely he would be watching my progress.

He put his arm around Mrs. Martin and gave her a kiss on the cheek. "Say hi to Fred, and give mom a big hug for me. I've got to be back in Billings tonight or I'd stop by." With that he was out the door. Shortly there was the sound of a car starting up and then he was gone.

Mrs. Martin gave me a shy smile "Sorry about the grilling, Jerry is my brother and has a doctorate in education; he designed your summer course from my suggestions."

After that we spent the next hour going over the study program for the summer.

CHAPTER 12

The summer went by very quickly. Ned and Henrietta helped me a lot in the beginning with the study program, but after the first month I was pretty much on my own. I would occasionally ask one of them about a social issue or anything dealing with people and places.

They weren't much help with the parts dealing with science and math though and I suspected that the course was only designed to familiarize me with the basics. Ned taught me how to work with money and after I had mastered that he showed me how their accounting system worked. He explained how the profit and loss columns worked and how to balance them with the income and expenses. I learned that in two days. The monetary system was decimal based and the coinage and paper currency was in several different multiples. It was mostly memorization. Then the dreaded day finally came.

The first day of school was on a Tuesday, and I was about to enter the first year of high school. Mrs. Martin and her brother spoke with the Johnsons and we decided to do the freshman year rather than have me bored to death with a hassle of younger eighth graders. I was fifteen and should be a sophomore, but they thought I would be too far behind in classes. Either way I was going to have to learn my way into the teenage culture of high school. We had worked out what classes I would take to minimize problems with teachers as well.

From the horror stories I had heard from the Johnson's on their years in high school, it was with nothing short of sheer terror that I faced that first day of high school; I was an outsider and would be treated as such until I had made a sort of 'rite of passage'.

Mrs. Martin gave me one last talking too, the day before. "Remember that your classmates don't know anything about you or where you come from. Some will welcome you, some will just avoid you, some will tolerate you, and others will try to take advantage of you. Be very careful to understand which are which, and try to respond with a positive attitude."

The next part I will always remember.

"The others to be wary of are the teachers."

That startled me, "the teachers?" I squeaked.

"Yes. There are some very good teachers in the school, but there are others that misuse it. I can't give names, but I'm sure you will find out just who is who before long, and, one last thing." She gave me a very solemn look. "Not only is Mr. Dressler the truancy officer, he is also the PE instructor." She saw the look of incomprehension on my face, "That's Physical Education. He has a tendency to be overbearing."

"Then I shouldn't hurt him too bad?"

I almost smiled at the look of shock on her face that slowly dawned into comprehension. "Just don't break anything, just bend him a little bit" she smiled mischievously.

"Yes ma'am" I replied with an understanding smile.

They didn't set my schedule up with PE for the first semester; I needed time to blend into the rest of the class. That was a big deal as there were only ten of us in the freshman class.

Nashua had only a small high school attached to the graded school which shared the gymnasium and cafeteria. I struggled early on with History, Civics, and English as the teacher, Ms. Graham thought I should know everything that all the rest of the class already knew.

Ms. Graham was an old gray haired spinster lady, as some of the kids called her, too mean to be able to keep a husband. Mrs. Martin had told me all about her though. Yes, she wasn't married, but she had been, to a Marine that didn't come back from the war in the Pacific. With that in mind I treated her with respect and she responded kindly and with encouragement.

One day, right after class, she asked me to stay behind for a moment. She had a request.

"Mr. Kingston? Would you mind doing a short talk on where you come from and what it was like before you came here?"

"I don't know Ms. Graham; it might take a little time to put everything together. Wouldn't you want to read it first?"

"That's very thoughtful Mr. Kingston; we could use it as the English composition requirement for this semester."

I agreed and headed off to my next class. I would have to be careful about the places I talked about, but by making the "King's Quest" as a place too far away from any large city with a common name might just work out.

Math was the last class of the day. It was rather boring, mostly just the four basic functions of addition, subtraction, multiplication, and division used in word problems. No rocket science there.

Mr. Hendricks was the Math teacher and he noticed my lack of enthusiasm for the assignments. He couldn't complain about my accuracy though, the only problem he marked off was because I forgot to put a comma in the result. After class he asked me to meet him in his office Wednesday morning during study hall.

I was fully prepared for one of those days when everything went wrong. Last week, one of the boys in the junior class had decided that I was to be his next target. I tried not to hurt him to bad and succeeded in making it look like it was all his fault. It earned us both a trip to see the principal, followed by a trip to see Mrs. Martin. After a proper scolding for both of us she let us return to class.

The door to Mr. Hendricks office was standing open when I got there, he waved me to come inside.

"Close the door and sit down Mr. Kingston" he said with a commanding voice, "we have some things to discuss."

"Yes, sir" was all I said as I sat down.

"Do you find my class boring?"

I had a hard time reading his face; it was just as impassive as Mrs. Martin's brother Jerry. "Ah, no sir."

His face clouded up. "When I ask you a direct question I expect a direct answer. Dr. Sanders tells me that you have a lot of potential and are probably being wasted sitting in my class."

I couldn't hold back the feeling of shock at what he had just said.

He smiled at me. "I can see very plainly that you are bored to tears. The only fault I could find with any of your work was the lack of a useless comma. Many places don't use a comma there either." He paused for a minute to collect his thoughts. "I hate to say it, but you don't belong in my class and you'd probably be as good at teaching it as I am."

I quickly shook my head no, no, no.

He was amused at that. "Alright, let's see what we

can do for you." He dug out a schedule of the math classes offered. "How are you at Trigonometry, Algebra, Geometry, and Calculus?"

"I don't recognize the names; can you give me an example?"

We spent the next two periods going over terminology and mathematical symbols before he was satisfied. He tossed the schedule aside. "I thought as much."

"Sir" I bolted upright, "I'm late for my next class"

"Which class is that?" he asked.

"Geography with Miss Wheeler" I replied.

"Don't worry about it, I'll talk to Sarah. We have a math club we're trying to start, would you be interested in joining?"

I told him I'd have to talk it over with my guardians, he said that was fine. As it turned out the math club was a flop, mostly from lack of interest. I wasn't too disappointed.

CHAPTER 13

Nashua is situated in the eastern half of Montana more a part of the central plains than the Rocky Mountains. As the weather was turning colder, clouds would roll in and rain would pour down before rolling right on out again. I was beginning to feel colder.

"Boy you sure are growing!" Henrietta gasped one morning as I appeared for breakfast. "Nedwick! We're going to have to go shopping, soon. His shoes are worn out and his pants are too short."

I'd already noticed that my arms seemed to stick out of my sleeves more than they used to.

"It's about time we made our annual pilgrimage anyway" Ned replied. "Is Becky expecting us?"

"Just got a letter from her yesterday, they'll be home waiting for us as usual. I also told her we were bringing Jason; they can't wait to meet him."

"I'll put up the sign and we can leave on Thursday night right after school gets out. We can show him what a big city looks like."

"Nedwick! He's probably seen bigger cities than Billings before."

She then explained to me that Becky was Ned's sister that lived in a small suburb outside of Billings. They tried to get together a couple of times a year, usually in the spring and fall. Since they had taken me in, the rest of the family wanted to meet the new relative, especially since I was European royalty. I cringed at what they were expecting from me.

"Besides we need to get you some new clothes. We may not live in the mountains, but winters can still be harsh if you don't have the right clothing. A few new shirts and pants, underwear, shoes and boots…Ned you better bring some money."

"Is there any way I can help pay for all of this?" I asked.

"Not unless you've a couple of gold bars on you" Ned replied. "Of course precious stones are good too…"

"Nedwick, get your mind off selling that shine. You start with that and the wrong type of people will start coming around."

I thought back about the personal possessions I had brought back from the flyer. There was the medallion that I had traded Arial for. I don't know where she had picked it up, but it didn't match her wardrobe. I don't know why I had kept it in the flyer. I went and dug it out of the box where I kept what few things I had.

"Is this worth anything?" I asked Henrietta.

She laid it on the kitchen table in the morning sun. "That is gorgeous Jason, where did you get it?"

"I traded with a girl for it before I came here. She told me it didn't fit with her wardrobe. Is it worth anything" I asked.

"I don't know" she replied. "My but it really is pretty, are you sure you want to part with it?"

"I'm sure. In fact, I'm giving it to you for all the wonderful things you've both done for me."

She stood up with it in her hands. I gently took it from her and placed the chain around her neck. The medallion lay perfectly beneath her throat.

"Oh, I couldn't, it's so beautiful and I have nowhere to wear it." Her actions belied her intense pleasure of the gift I had bestowed upon her.

Ned just winked at me.

The trip to Billings was interesting, to say the least, It was the first chance I had to see what their cities looked like. They bought me a lot of new clothes and a new pair of shoes and boots. Ned's sister's family really made me feel welcome, and their young children did too. I was now cousin Jason; and it felt good.

CHAPTER 14

First semester ended with excellent marks in all but History. I was beginning to catch on to the English grammar rules, their exceptions, and really wondered how anyone could keep it all straight. The Johnson's were understandably proud of me and I was actually getting used to things as they were. It had helped to keep me occupied while I waited for word from mom and dad. If all went according to plan I should be hearing from them somewhere around their first breakout point in about two months. Somehow, I'd have to get back to the flyer and check. That should be easy, all I had to do was wait until the preserves were getting low and sweet talk Henrietta into picking up some more.

We did make it out to the farm again just before it got very cold. The storm two days before had dropped six inches of snow and the roads weren't very good, but the temperature was back up into the fifties so most of it would melt by mid-day.

Ned's brother Jeff had been out to make sure all of the pipes were drained and the water shut off, but I was a little concerned that the cold temperatures would freeze all the contents of the cellar. I could tell that Henrietta was thinking the same thing. The house had been occupied last winter; just having someone living there had kept the cellar warm enough to prevent things from freezing as the Barton's had moved away this past spring.

"It would be such a shame to see them freeze and go to waste" she lamented. "Ned, we're just going to have to make more room in the storeroom for as much of this as we can. Maybe we could borrow Jeff's truck while the weather is still good?"

The next day, with Jeff's help, the three of us loaded all of the preserves into his truck. Ned asked if it would be alright if he gave Jeff some of the Hooch for his help. I reluctantly agreed; if Henrietta ever found out we'd both be in deep trouble.

I had the only key, and while they were both loading the last boxes into the back of the truck, I picked four jars out of the storeroom and put them into a small box. I then took the box upstairs and picked out from the closets a few more things that looked like they would fit me.

Ned gave me a questioning look when I brought the box out, I gave him a quick smile and put the box in the truck. I would give them to him after we got all of the other stuff from the cellar put away.

When we got back to the store, we carried the boxes down to the lower storeroom and put them in the corner Ned had cleared out. I had discovered another little spot where they let me keep my really personal stuff. In here I put two of the jars. Later after we were finishing up, I secretly gave Ned the other two. He thanked me and sent me upstairs to let Henrietta know we were done unloading. While I was gone he secretly cached one of the jars and gave the other to Jeff. By then she had come down and quickly put several of the jars of preserves into an empty box and had me take it out to Jeff in thanks for his help. Jeff went home a happy man in more ways than one.

CHAPTER 15

The first semester ended and the school closed down for Christmas break. I had studied the aspects of what this holiday meant to some people, and I could see both the good aspects to what it stood for and the downside as well. I had to tread a fine line on the subject as some people just didn't understand that not everyone believed in the same things as they did. Misunderstandings could lead to dire results.

The second half of my freshman year started off about the same, English, History, Math and Science as before, but this time I had to take PE. Mr. Dressler was the PE instructor and I dreaded having to deal with him.

Over the break I had had a talk with Mrs. Martin. She told me I was assimilating quite nicely, but there was no way I could avoid taking PE this semester.

"You might be able to get excused from it if you were on one of the athletic teams however, but the only one going right now is basketball; the coach is Mr. Randall."

Mr. Randall was also the biology teacher but not enough students took Biology so he coached the athletic teams as well. Mr. Dressler was only a part time teacher and full time truant officer.

I had spent part of the summer reading up on the various school sports, Baseball during the summer months, Football in the fall, Basketball and Hockey during the winter months. I decided I'd try out if I could. On weekends Ned had showed me the mechanics of how to shoot, he had a hoop mounted on the garage over the doors. I enjoyed the time we spent together, I felt sad that they hadn't been able to have their own children; he would have been a great father.

I wouldn't be able to try out for the team until the week after school started so I was stuck with PE until then. I was going to have to deal with Mr. Dressler.

All of the freshman and sophomore boys took PE together; the girls were exempt from such gross and disgusting things. I got along well with all of my classmates and had one small clash with one of the other freshman boys. Yes, none other than Randall Dressler, Mr. Dressler's son.

This was going to be ugly. It reminded me of when I first started studying unarmed combat at the Bergenhaumen School back on Evenset. I had also studied celestial mechanics and cosmic navigation. That was only two years ago but it felt like it was long ago and far away and in another lifetime.

Fourth period was just before lunch, and we were all lined up in the small gymnasium attached to the side of the cafeteria. "A motley group of misfits if I ever saw one" I thought. This was definitely a classic example of why one size does not fit all. There were nine of us and we ranged in size from short and fat, to tall and skinny, or short and skinny, to tall and fat. I fit somewhere in the middle.

"All right ladies, we're going to do some real simple stuff here" He started off with. "First I want you to pair off, first one from each end come here. One of you two, take a mat off the pile over there and find a nice comfy spot. At the end of class the other one will put it back. Next two, do the same." This continued until there were three of us left, Randall was on one end and me on the other. The poor kid in the middle was Walter Webster.

"Walter, you pair-off with me, go grab a mat." He turned to me with a wicked smile on his face. "Kingston, go grab a mat." Walter and I did as told.

"OK ladies, now we're going to do 20 sit ups, your partner will hold your feet down then you switch positions. Begin."

This went fine and twenty minutes later everyone had completed their set.

"Next set is 20 push-ups, everyone down on your hands."

I finished up just ahead of Randall and stood up

just ahead of him. As I looked down the line I could see that the rest were still trying. I hadn't even worked up a sweat yet. Just then the bell rang to end the class.

"Ladies! Don't forget to hang up your mats, and then grab a shower."

I checked the time, if we did that we'd never make it in time for lunch, I decided to skip the shower, quickly changed clothes and headed to the line going in the door.

"Kingston! Where are you going?" Mr. Dressler hollered. "I told you to hang up the mat."

"No sir" I hollered back from the hallway, "you told us that one person gets the mat the other one hangs it up." Then the door closed between us. As I turned around I almost ran into Mr. Randall.

"Well hello there Mr. Kingston. I understand you would like to join the basketball team."

Before he could continue the gym door slammed open and Mr. Dressler stomped out. With no regard for any of the other people in the hallway, he pushed his way over to me and grabbed me by the arm. Before he could go anywhere Mr. Randall stepped in front of him.

"What's going on here?" he ordered. By then several of the other teachers had gathered around.

Dressler got into Mr. Randall's face and told him to stay out of it. I hadn't been excused from class yet. Mr. Randall didn't move.

Mrs. Martin calmly stepped in. "Let's move this

into the gym, we don't need this disruption out here in the hallway. Everyone go about your own business now" as she shooed everyone else away from the gym door.

Inside the gym nearly all of the other students had left except for Randall who was still standing over by the mat.

"All right Dressler" she steamed at him, "what's this all about?"

"Kingston here was leaving without permission. I was just bringing him back in here to finish what he was told to do."

"Jason? Is this true?" She gave me a dark look; I couldn't tell what she was thinking.

"Ma'am, he paired us off to do setups and pushups, one of the partners would get the mat, the other would put it back. I picked it up so it was up to Randall to put it back."

"Jason, I told you at the beginning of school that some times what you say could have dire consequences." She then turned to Dressler, "Is what he just said true?"

"Now see here…" Dressler started to say.

"Mr. Randall, what is your schedule like?"

"I have a Biology class right after lunch" he replied.

"Then you should probably leave. I'll take care of this."

Mr. Randall reluctantly left leaving only the four of us standing alone in the gym. My stomach growled.

"Boys it's getting late, you get off to lunch, and right

after your last period, I expect to see both of you in my office before you go home." She took a quick look at Mr. Dressler first. "Boys, you're excused."

Randall and I left quietly, and since we were the last ones in line, we ate together. After a little coaxing I got him to talking. I don't remember exactly what we talked about, but I got the impression he didn't have to many friends. I could understand that with a father like that.

CHAPTER 16

After last period we met again at Mrs. Martin's office. She quizzed us both about what happened in class but I don't think she learned much. She dismissed us and Randall and I walked home from school as far as the turnoff to the road he lived on, I walked on from there alone crossing the tracks behind the store. The train wouldn't be coming through town until later tonight.

Henrietta met me at the top of the stairs with a stern look. Man, was I in for it, but she didn't say anything except that Ned needed me in the storeroom. I quickly put my books in my room changed clothes and went downstairs to the storeroom.

When Ned had a minute he stepped into the doorway and asked me what had happened. Henrietta had told him that the school had called and I was being held after class and would be home a little late.

I gave him a brief overview and he just nodded. "Bound to happen sooner or later. Hate it that it was you that got caught in it though."

I sensed that there was more to this than just what happened today but I didn't ask.

"Had a truck come in early, he just left most of it inside the door" as he handed me the packing slips, "Shouldn't take you to long. Going to be dark early tonight, I'm going to close up in about an hour; you should be done by then." Then he left me alone with the shipment and my thoughts.

I took care of the shipment and stocked the shelves. By that time Ned had locked the doors and we headed upstairs for supper.

The meal was quiet and passed quickly. After we had cleared the table and settled into the living room Henrietta asked me to tell them what had happened at school. I told them everything exactly as it had happened. Henrietta was furious, but Ned looked like he was deep in thought.

"One of these days he's going to get his comeuppance" she sputtered.

"Let's not be too hasty dear" he replied, "I think that there's more to this than what we're seeing." Sometimes Ned could be quite cryptic.

If there was more to this, it would have to include things that I wouldn't know about. "What do you know about the Dressler's Ned?" I asked him.

"He grew up around here, Henrietta and I have known the family for about ten years now. He was passed over during the war, something about a problem with his right ear. His wife Jenna is from Wyoming, I've no idea how they met, and their kids were always a little strange."

"I don't think Randall is strange. He doesn't have any friends but it's not his fault, I kind of like him. I don't know who is sister is though, she's in the seventh grade I think."

"Yes she is, Jason" Henrietta said, "And I think it's nice of you to make friends with him. Just don't rile up his father though, that could lead to trouble."

"How'd he get to be Truant Officer?"

"Simple enough" Ned replied, "He's the only one that applied for it."

"Mrs. Martin said something about trouble with a girl a while back?" I was fishing, hoping for anything they'd give me.

Henrietta gave me a strange look, like I'd dug something out of the ground and it didn't smell good. "That would be the Colliers little girl."

For a moment I thought she wasn't going to tell me anything more.

"Mrs. Martin got in a little too deep on that one. She tries to save any stray that comes along, just like you were when they found you at the farm. Poor little girl was taken in by the Webster's when her parents divorced. Her father ran off to Billings and her mother committed suicide. She was doing all right until she went berserk one day in school and nearly beat the teacher to death before running off into the woods. The teacher survived but when they found her in the woods Mr. Dressler kept the others from just plain shooting her on sight. They said she'd gone mad."

I watched a tear slowly roll down her cheek.

"Mr. Dressler managed to get her constrained and put her in a jail cell. The deputy on duty that night fell asleep and the next morning they found she had hung herself in the cell. The deputy was fired for dereliction of duty and Mrs. Martin blames Mr. Dressler for her death. Worst of all, little Rowena Collier was Judith Martin's niece."

Perhaps things are not what they always seem to be, even in this little rural corner of Montana. And why am I here? Because of the Queryl? I wonder.

Next week I tried out for the basketball team but didn't make it. I was discouraged and didn't speak to Randall for a week. Ned gave me a pep talk, as he called it, and I made up with Randall. That didn't mean I got along any better with his father though, I still had to go to PE.

CHAPTER 17

I spent the next summer working in the store with Ned. I unloaded the trucks, stocked the shelves, and carried the customer's purchases out to their vehicle. It didn't take long to get to know all of his customers and what their needs were. It was fairly boring work, but I didn't mind, it made the time go by.

Most evenings Randall and I would play basketball out back of the store until dark. Later on a couple of the other guys would stop by. First was Larry Burke, he was a junior. Then Larry brought along Ted Langdon and before long we had to move over to the playground. That's when Mr. Randall showed up.

By the time school began we had a full team that had been practicing all summer long, and I had my next run in with Mr. Dressler. It was Tuesday afternoon and I was rummaging in my locker for my math book when I heard the voice that I had been dreading.

"Kingston? Why weren't you in PE class today" he

was standing just outside the gym doors not more than ten feet from me.

"Basketball team members don't take PE" I replied, a little unsure of myself, "it's in the school regulations." You could have heard a pin drop in the hallway; nobody said a word, just waiting to see what would happen next.

He stared at me stonily for what seemed an eternity before a slow grin crept over his face. "Kingston, my boy, you've worked out well. Randall likes you and you've fit into the community like you grew up here." He walked up close and stuck out his hand and clapped me on the back all the while whispering in my ear "But I know there are still some secrets you're hiding. There better not be bad things following you or there will be consequences." Another smile and he walked away.

Slowly the conversations in the hallway came back to normal and I quietly closed my locker and headed to math class; I was a little shaky and drenched in sweat.

The rest of that school year passed without incident. At least once a month I would head out to the farm to check on things, at least until the weather turned real cold. I had seen these contraptions, as Ned called them, in the Montgomery Ward catalog, which let you walk on top of the snow. The catalog listed them as Snow Shoes and they were priced reasonably, so I asked Ned about buying them. He told me he didn't think that I would get enough use out of them, and the farm would be just fine until the weather cleared in the springtime.

Of course when Christmas time came around, they were sitting on the floor beside our little tree in the corner of the living room. We didn't buy a lot of presents, but the last time we had visited Ned's sister Becky in Billings I gave her enough money to buy both Ned and Henrietta a nice present. It arrived by mail the first part of December along with a letter showing me what she had bought them. I wrote her a letter back and thanked her.

CHAPTER 18

My sophomore year had been mostly uneventful, two of our classmates had moved out of state, and one of them was Betsy Warren. I had just gotten to know her and was thinking of asking her out when her father went to work in another state. I felt really depressed for a week or so before Randall wanted me to join their little baseball group.

Ned had mentioned baseball but he had never been interested in it. Randall started to teach me how to catch and throw the ball back. Hitting the ball was another matter entirely. He would toss the ball into the air beside him and as it came down he would swing the bat and knock it out onto the field. At first he would just hit it out and I would run to catch it. There were just so many things that I had never had a chance at learning while living in a spaceship, even running and jumping. Just isn't any room for that sort of thing.

Ned had started having me wait on customers and

ring up their purchases. He told me that they appreciated accuracy and honesty. If you made a mistake in their favor they might not say anything about it, but if you made an error that cost them money they would be most irate about it.

He told me "Best to do it right the first time! That way there'll be no problems."

That made a lot of sense, I told him, and always checked my figures twice. Then one day old Mr. Grappart came in and wanted to know how much it was for two dozen jars of tomato soup. I knew we didn't have that many but I told him that we could order it up and it would be here in two to three days. I also gave him the same price as if it was off the shelf. He said that was fine and left. I assumed that it would be alright to go ahead and add them to our next order.

Two days later the two dozen cans of tomato soup showed up and I called Mr. Grappart to tell him he could pick them up anytime. I was shocked to hear him tell me that he had changed his mind. I was devastated and couldn't think how I was going to explain it to Ned.

"That's why you always get a deposit on an unusual order like that" he told me. "Don't worry son, we'll sell them eventually, and don't tell anyone else, they'll think we'll sell them at a cheaper price just to unload them. They're not perishable, just put them in the lower storeroom with the rest of the soups." I had to make other similar special orders, but I always cleared it with Ned first before placing the order.

CHAPTER 19

School started again that following fall, another uneventful year. I was getting better marks and was almost at the top of my class. My Junior year was going just as spectacularly as the previous year. But the summer before my senior year was different. The winter snows had not been as deep and the rivers were running a lot lower than in many years. I learned a new term, drought!

Most all of my income comes from renting out the farms fields to the neighboring farmers for growing crops and cutting hay. It was going to be a lean year for the farmers and with Ned's advice we cut the rents to help them out as much as we could. They were appreciative, but for Ed Crowell it wasn't enough and he went bankrupt.

Later on that summer the bank foreclosed and sold off his farm, all of his stock, and most of the farm equipment to pay off his mortgage. The Crowell's eventually moved back east to Ohio where his brother lived and he took a job in a steel mill; he had a wife and four small children to feed. One of the kids at school said his mom had gotten a letter from Mrs. Crowell and that they were doing well. I still felt somewhat bad for them though.

With Ned's wise advice my bank account had been steadily growing. The taxes were still more than covered by leasing out the use of the farm's fields to the local farmers.

After that first year with Ned and Henrietta I had spent a day out at the farm building a wall in front of the flyer. It was built like a pair of doors, but fit against the side walls. From the outside it looked like it was a solid wall. On the inside it was latched to the upper beam as well as the floor with a bar across to keep them from moving. To get inside I cut a rough door on the further side. It wasn't much but the best I knew how and it would have to do until I had more time.

CHAPTER 20

The summer ended as all summers do and before I knew it, it was a bright fall day and the first day of school. But what made it really special, this was my senior year at Nashua High School. I thought back over the last three years and wondered where it had all gone. My life before that was beginning to become more of a dream than reality, but I still held to the thought that mom and dad would be coming back for me.

Periodically over the last two years I had to meet with Mrs. Martin and sometimes her brother Dr. Jerry Sanders would be there as well. During these meetings she would ask how I was doing, if I was having troubles in school and how I was getting along with the Johnsons.

I knew she had access to all of my test scores and was probably receiving reports from the teachers as well. She told me that they were both pleased with my progress and to keep up the good work.

"It will work out well for you in the future" she told

me. I really didn't realize the full import of what she had said until much later.

Jerry sometimes brought along a little test he would like me to take. I would struggle through them sometimes completely baffled by the questions. He never told me what the results were, even when I asked him; he just smiled and said they were experimental and he would share the results as soon as he figured out what they were. From the way he smiled when he said it, I knew I would never find out.

But, other than that, my senior year was turning out to be just as uneventful as the previous three years had been. Somehow I had managed to hide myself in plain sight camouflaged as a normal high school student. I was beginning to wonder who was I really hiding from? That was what really bothered me the most.

CHAPTER 21

And then in a flash, my senior year was almost over and graduation was only a few weeks away. Graduation time is such a solemn occasion. Over the last four years I had made many new friends and learned so much about this small community. I was going to hate to leave when the time came. Maybe Arson could come up with an extraction procedure that would make things easy all the way around. But for Ned and Henrietta I didn't think it would be easy. They had become my surrogate parents for the last four years.

Somewhere within the next year I should get confirmation when Mom, Dad, and Dora had returned. But Dora would be nearly grown up by now, I would hardly know her. I wondered if she would even remember me?

Feelings of frustration came over me; I was going to have strong words with Arson for using me as a bargaining point so that they could return to the derelict. Arial has probably been married off and I'd never see her again.

Somehow that made me very sad. I realized that she was a few years older, but I still held hope that somehow she would come to like me. Yes, she had acted like a spoiled brat, but one of the nicest looking red headed spoiled brats I'd ever met. And I missed her terribly, even more than Betsy Warren. Why does the past always cling to you like that?

I had learned early on that the top student scholastically was expected to give a speech during the graduation ceremony. I just wanted to get good marks, but keep out of notice. Holly Thatcher, however, was almost a perfect student with straight A's. By carefully manipulating my marks I managed to stay a point behind her; and I almost got away with it.

"Jason" a mild contralto voice called from behind me as I was heading home after school, "Wait up for me." Holly was dark haired, about five foot tall plus a couple of inches, a little over weight for her height, but she was smart and I avoided her like the plague.

"Hi, Holly." I stopped and waited for her to catch up with me. "Congratulations on Valedictorian, your parents should be pleased."

"Not really, they just want me to marry one of the local blockheads and start having babies. They've got it all planned out, they want lots of grandchildren."

She sounded real down about it.

I looked down at her. When we were freshman we were the about same height, I had grown nearly a foot taller since then. She had seemed really shy back then and I didn't want to get involved.

"Holly you've got a great opportunity here. You should apply to colleges; I know you'll get accepted." I tried to sound upbeat. "Get out there and make something of yourself girl."

She perked up a little bit. "First, I think you should write one great speech, I'll help you if you want, and think positive."

What had I just said? Alarm bells started ringing in my head.

She looked up at me and with a big smile, "Would you really help me with my speech?"

I gulped. She was not only smart, she was downright cunning. I'll have to be careful around her. "Of course I will, what works for you?" I started backpedaling but I felt like I was over the edge already.

"It will work better if I come over to your place" she replied eagerly, "my family would be all over you." She looked at me expectantly. "How about right now?"

Trap sprung. "I don't think so Holly, I have to work in the store after school."

"What do you do in the store?" she asked moving closer to me.

"Trucks come in nearly every day; I'll be unpacking and stocking the shelves for the next hour or so."

"Tomorrow night then?" she waited breathlessly.

"I'll let you know tomorrow."

She pouted a little before turning and walking away.

"Boy you sure don't know much about girls do you?" Billy Thatcher remarked. Billy was a junior, and Holly's younger brother. He had joined the basketball team this past year and was better at it than I was. "You are messing with fire with that one." He was wiggling his fingers as if burnt just to make his point.

"She will suck you in and spit you out, just ask Randall Dressler. He took a shine to her back in eighth grade and she messed him up royally." He looked up at the weather coming in from the west. "Umm, could be a storm coming and I don't just mean Holly either. Word of advice?" he posed to me.

"In this case anything to avoid another confrontation like that one" I replied.

"Well, best I can see it, you've got three options." He looked at me with a big grin on his face. I knew him well enough to know that I wasn't going to like any one of them.

"First, you can take your chances and help her out, and by the way she won't need any help with her speech, she's already got it written."

"She's what?!" I exclaimed.

"Yeah, she wrote it last year and been revising it ever since. Don't believe that malarkey she gave you about being married off, she's already been accepted to Montana

State." He must have noted the look of shock on my face.

"Second, you could run off with the gypsies and never come back. Personally, I like that one the best. Or…"

"Or what, shoot myself?"

"Not quite, do what she wants, turn it around and back her into a corner. I'll bet you she'll run."

I gulped at the last one, but considering the alternatives, the best defense is a good offense. I think Coach Randall taught us that one.

"Ah, thanks Billy, I'll go shoot myself now."

We both laughed as we headed home in opposite directions.

CHAPTER 22

There wasn't as much stock waiting for me as I thought there would, only took me an hour to get it all taken care of and the paper work filed. I had been doing nearly all of the paper work for the past two years anyway. I washed my hands off in the storeroom sink and went out front to see if Ned needed any help.

There was only one woman up front talking to Ned and she only had a couple of bags on the counter in front of her. Wouldn't hurt to offer my services though, I thought.

"Ah, there you are. All finished out back?" Ned asked me.

I nodded and turned to find that the woman was Holly's mother. "Would you like a hand with your bags Mrs. Thatcher?" I asked.

"That would be nice of you Jason, besides I need to talk to you" she looked over at Ned who had a questioning look on his face, "in private if you please."

"Of course" I replied and picked up the bags and

headed out the door.

She opened the back door of the car and I put them on the floor so they wouldn't tip over. "Will that be all ma'am?" I asked.

"I'll be blunt young man" she began, "Holly has worked hard for her marks and now she has a college scholarship. I wouldn't want anything to get in the way of her going to college if you get what I mean?"

"But all I did was offer to help with her speech!" I stammered.

"Are you sure about that? Just to be safe it's best you two maintain a distance, understood?"

I smiled back at her. "Yes ma'am, stay away from Holly, not a problem, and thank you for that."

"Odd, you look relieved." She searched my face. "Yes, I do believe you are relieved." Then she chuckled. "Oh, that little minx; don't worry Jason, I'll speak to her."

I watched as she drove away thinking about what Billy had told me about her and Randall. Does the daughter take after the mother? Poor Randall.

Ned gave me a curious look when I went back in the store but he didn't ask and I didn't volunteer. Henrietta was another matter however; she wanted all the details before asking me if I had learned my lesson. I'm not totally sure what lesson she meant, but it must have to do with girls I guess, just leave them alone.

CHAPTER 23

A few days later we were settled in the living room listening to the news when, during a commercial, Henrietta asked if I'd heard anything back on the colleges I'd applied to.

"I've gotten three replies, one goes in the trash immediately" I replied.

"Let me guess" Ned laughed, "Montana State."

Henrietta gave him a very withering look.

"Made any decisions on what career path?" Ned asked.

"I had thought some about just staying here and working in the store for a year or so" I mused. Truthfully I hadn't seriously thought about going anywhere.

"Tell you what Jason" Ned began, "There's one more option. You could always join the army or the National Guard. But, if you don't go to college, before long they are going to draft you anyway. So if you're not sure about college, join one of the military services for four years, get that obligation out of the way, then you can use the GI bill to help you pay for college."

I told him I'd think about it.

"May I take the afternoon off after school?" I asked, "I haven't checked on the farm in a while and maybe I can think while I'm up there."

"Sure, come see me when you get home, and before you leave."

The next day was the first time in a long time that I had walked home from school alone. There were only two weeks of school left, and most of the seniors were heading off to this college or that one. The others were even going into the military or farming. Even if I stayed here and didn't get drafted, most of my friends would be gone. It was a hard decision, but there were plans that were already in the works.

It was only a few miles out to the farm. I rode slowly as I wasn't in any hurry and there weren't any cars on the road; not that there ever were this far back. I parked the bike in the bushes beside the barn and slowly walked around the building.

I had been coming out here at least several times every year and more often during the summer months. I had gotten a bicycle my first Christmas and it had taken me several weeks to learn to ride that thing. But since then I nearly wore it out exploring around the area and spending time up here at the farm. It was so quiet and peaceful out here.

Almost reluctantly I unlocked the barn door and snuck into the flyer. Sitting in the pilots chair brought back old memories. Sometimes I almost wondered if they were real, but who else around here has a spaceship in their barn? To conserve power I completely power the flyer down before I leave each time.

While the systems were coming online I thought about what I should do next year. That was going to be a tough choice to leave here and…"

"Beep, Beep, Beep!"

I sat bolt upright, three incoming messages. I sat there undecided what to do. Almost dreading what it might say, I keyed the receiver and glanced at the messages waiting for me. The first was from Arson, a new protocol. I skipped over that one. The second was from dad.

I dove into that one and read it twice. They had managed to outrun the Queryl and landed safely at our home world of Evenset. They had immediately present-ed all of their materials on the derelict and sat back and watched as the council wrangled over how to handle it. It was like all the old naysayers were back in power again.

When they were finally able to convince enough supporters that it was a worthwhile effort to investigate the dormant ship, it was another battle for them to get in-cluded in the mission.

"Mom knows that you are unable to send a reply,

but know that we all love you and will be coming for you soon."

The third message was from Arial? I still had her father's message to read, but this one intrigued me.

"Jasom" she began, "I know you've been abandoned on what could very well be a hostile planet, but I hope you're doing well. Dad said that he'd done what he could to get you situated where you would be safe. Lately I have been listening to their conversations when they don't know I'm there and I believe that you were placed there on purpose. Your sister and I have been closer since you've been gone and we've come up with a theory."

The message wasn't that long, but she put a lot of scary stuff in there. Her last comment was that she truly believed that we would meet again. I had to dry my eyes several times. I didn't really feel like reading Arson's message, but I printed it out along with the other two. Maybe later I could read more into it than what was written there.

Regretfully I powered the flyer down and was just about to step out from behind the screen hiding it, when I heard voices.

CHAPTER 24

"It's got to be around here somewhere, we've been through the house and the only place left is the barn." I didn't recognize the voice. "Anything up above?"

I quietly slipped back over to the flyers hatch as I heard footsteps overhead. I made sure the hatch was locked so only I could get in.

"Nah! Nothing up here but old moldy hay. Doesn't look like anyone's been up here in years." I could hear him coming down the stairs just outside my hiding place. I didn't recognize his voice either. "Where's Hawthorne?" the latest voice asked.

"He went down into the lower level, should be right back...yeah, here he comes now."

"What's down there Hawthorne?" the first voice asked.

"Nothin' down there chief; doesn't look like old Barton ever used it. You don't suppose it's hidden in the house?"

"If it is, he hid it well."

I stopped listening and slipped back toward the back wall, the single small window near the ceiling let in just enough light to see by. I stumbled and almost cried out. I poked around with my foot and found something underneath the cover of hay.

I quickly brushed the hay away from a handle set in the floor. It was a trap door down into the lower level. Quickly I brushed all the hay from around the edge and slowly pulled it open. I listened then stole a quick look; there was no one down there. It was a good thing I had put a lock on the inside of the boards that let into here, they wouldn't be able to get into here with it locked.

Quietly I dropped down to the floor below and with the aid of a long pole I was able to close the trap door. From here I would have to be very careful not to be seen. Gently I opened a window and slipped into the bushes out of sight, closing the window behind me.

I crept through the bushes around to where I could see the three men standing by the side door to the house. I couldn't tell how they had gotten it open; I was more interested in getting out of there. It was a good thing I had parked the bike in the bushes, they hadn't found it yet. I grabbed the bike and headed out beyond the barn keeping it between me and them until I got beyond the fence line. From there I headed back to the main road.

When I got to the road I could see their vehicle in

the driveway. In the gathering twilight I could read the license plate and make of the car, but the color was a little dubious, some dark color, could have been brown, blue or black.

I headed home as fast as that bike would go. When I got home I quickly put the bike in the garage out of sight and closed the door behind me.

"Well son, did you get your thinking done?" Ned said casually.

"Ahhhh!" I nearly jumped out of my skin. "You startled me!" I cried.

"You alright Jason, you look like you've seen a ghost? What's going on?"

I leaned up against the side of the garage and Ned got a worried look on his face. I told him everything that I'd seen, minus what I was really out there for.

"And you got the license plate?" he asked eagerly?

I nodded, "and the make and model, but couldn't tell the color in the darkness:

"Come on" he grabbed my arm and we headed across the road to Hiram Wheeler's place.

CHAPTER 25

He beat on the door until Hiram finally came to the door. "Ned? Ned Johnson?" He saw the looks on our faces and he quickly looked up and down the road wondering what the calamity was. "What's got you boys all worked up, somebody been killed? Henrietta's all right isn't she?"

"Can we come in Hiram? This is an emergency!" Ned stammered.

"Sure, sure, let's go into my office" as he ushered us into one of the rooms in the front of the house.

We sat in bare wooden office chairs while Hiram sat down behind his desk. I'd never been in his house before, I just knew he was retired and lived alone. While Ned filled him in on what I'd seen, I looked at some of the citations hanging on his walls. Hiram was a retired state trooper!

"Tell me exactly what you heard and saw Jason" Hiram commanded.

I went over every detail I could remember, all I said was that I was hiding in a secluded walkway that they couldn't see easily. That there were three of them that I knew of and one of them was called chief and another Hawthorne. I'd crawled through the bushes and saw that they'd broken into the house before grabbing my bike and fleeing home. Then Ned brought me over here.

I calmed down for a minute before asking "Do you have any idea who these people are?"

"I'll look into it" he replied calmly, "but for now don't say anything to anyone."

"But what about Henrietta?" Ned asked.

"The less she knows the better, I have a good idea who they are but let's keep it quiet for now."

Ned didn't budge, just sat there waiting for him to say something more. "That's not good enough," he finally managed to get out. "I'm not one of your trooper under-lings."

Hiram just sat there for a moment looking a little exasperated. He must have been tough on those that had to work for him.

"Very well then, on your head shall it be. Your descriptions, Jason, match with a group of people that the agency has been watching for several years now. I still have a few friends that keep me up to date on what's going on, provided I let them know when something useful pops up around here."

"What were they looking for, the Hooch?" I said without realizing it.

"Just what do you know about Hooch?" Hiram asked suspiciously.

"Well" I thought fast, "I inherited the farm when my family passed away and since I've come to live with Ned and Henrietta everyone in town's been telling me how Mr. Barton used to make the best Hooch in the county." I noticed that Ned's face had softened.

"We've been all over that place, and there's no working still anywhere that we've found" Ned continued. "And why show up four years later? That don't make any sense at all."

Hiram's chair squeaked as he leaned back. "You are right there, it doesn't make any sense, unless…" he seemed lost in thought for a moment, "Lets say we just keep this all quiet for now. Let me do some checking around."

"Isn't someone going to go out and arrest them for breaking into my house?" I cried.

"Sorry son" Hiram replied with an expansive gesture around him, "I'm retired. And, by the time the local sheriff could get out there they'd be gone anyway. "I suggest you go back in the morning and put some new locks on the doors.

Somewhat dejectedly we left Hiram sitting in his office and made our way back across the street to our house. We were going to get grilled by Henrietta when we got upstairs, but there was nothing more that could be done tonight.

I'm not sure if she believed us, but Ned told her that I had some questions regarding the safety of the farm so they had paid a visit to Hiram Wheeler. He told us to put new locks on the doors so they would be doing that tomorrow.

"Well, I suppose I could put together a picnic basket and we could enjoy the early spring."

CHAPTER 26

I bought all of the locks that Ned carried in the store and the next afternoon we went out and installed them. I walked around the outside of the house and found where someone had forced a window into the kitchen. Inside all of the cupboards had been emptied and upstairs all of the drawers pulled out and the contents dumped on the floor. If they had been looking for a still, they hadn't found it, and this was just wanton destruction.

I walked back down the stairs and down the back hall to the kitchen. When I got there I saw a stranger standing in the doorway. "What do you want?" I hollered at him.

"Calm down son, I'm Lt. Samuel Drake of the Montana State police. Are you Jason Kingston? I'm told you have had a break in."

"Yes sir, I'm Jason Kingston and this is my farm. Someone forced this window over here" I pointed to the window beside me, "And dumped everything on the floor. I indicated the heaps of things scattered across the floor.

"Was anyone hurt during this burglary? Do you know if anything is missing?"

He was writing notes in a little brown book as he asked the questions.

"From all of this clutter I wouldn't be able to tell. It looks more like they did this for spite than anything else."

I could see he sensed the bitterness in my words.

"Any idea what they were looking for?"

"I don't know, truthfully I'm not even sure if I'd known anyway, I've only lived around here for a few years and most of that with the Johnson's."

"You don't live here?"

"No, I inherited the place when my family passed away and I was placed as a foster child with the Johnson's." I just then remembered to look around for them.

"Don't worry son, they're waiting outside, I've already spoken with them. Mrs. Johnson seemed a little upset about all of this. Do you know why?"

A ghost of a smile crossed my face. "Probably because I didn't say anything to her about any of this; Hiram said not to. He's the one that called you isn't he?"

"He was my commander several years ago before he retired. He was one of the toughest bosses I've ever had, but straight as an arrow. I've learned a lot from him."

I looked around at the devastation. "What am I supposed to do now?"

"Do what you can. Pick it all up, new locks, have

someone come through more often. All things you can do, none of them come with guarantees. Or, you could sell the place..." He replied noncommittally.

He motioned me outside and we went out to talk with the Ned and Henrietta

It took nearly two weeks to clean everything up and get ready for graduation too. I had put off any decision while the farm issue was in the air. Slowly things settled back into a semblance of normalcy. I had managed to avoid a conflict with Holly thanks to the quick advice of her cousin and her mother giving her a good talking too. She still flirted with me in the hallways, but I'd just smile back and walk away. At least that's how things went until the last day of school.

CHAPTER 27

I'd just handed in the last of my textbooks and was cleaning out the last of my accumulated junk from my locker. Anything left over that I wanted went in my pack. Whatever was left in the lockers after that would be cleaned out by the custodial staff during the summer. I closed the door with a sigh.

"It wasn't that bad was it?" Holly asked from behind me.

I paused for a moment to calm my thoughts before turning around and looking down at her. Funny, she didn't look so short today. And a little slimmer too as I gazed at her standing before me. Then I noticed the high heels.

"Must be something I ate, or didn't eat?" she said with a saucy smile on her face. "You like?" then she did a quick pirouette.

"You look really nice Holly" I said earnestly, "and you're going to wow them with your speech as well I bet."

"Why thank you Jason. It's very nice of you to say

so."

She looked like she had something she wanted to say but wasn't sure how to do it without causing embarrassment, probably to herself more than me.

"I'm sorry about how I treated you the other day, I was mad at you. Then mother spoke to me and I got madder yet."

"Just spit it out Holly, what are you trying to say?"

"That I finally realized that you were actually holding back on your marks because you didn't want to be noticed. I thought you were making fun of me by letting me have the higher marks and then offering to help with my speech. I struck back the only way I know how."

"Well, you're right on one thing, I was holding back because I didn't want to be in the spotlight, you're much better at it than I am. It hasn't been easy for me you know. I had a lot to learn the first two years just to catch up with the rest of the class. But you did earn it, and you would have been there even if I hadn't come along."

"Jason, I know that's not the only thing, what are you hiding from?"

"Holly, I am an orphan. Abandoned here with not much more than my name and the clothes I was wearing at the time. I survived by eating preserves from the jar and cooking rats and mice that I could catch in the field before Mrs. Martin and Mr. Dressler found me. I grew up in a place that would be as equally strange to you if you had been thrust into it as I have been here. The Johnsons have been wonderful to me and I now find myself in a position where I have to make a very difficult decision."

"Well my friend, I can call you a friend still can't I?" she was totally casual about it.

I just nodded.

"Let's walk" as she took my hand and we casually strolled down to the corner talking. From there her house was in the other direction from mine so we talked for quite a while before saying goodbye.

That one short talk was enough to clear the air between us, but I realized that I still had to be careful around her; I believe that anyone was fair game for her.

"See you tomorrow and don't forget about the party afterwards." she waved and walked away.

That had seemed like a normal conversation, especially as it was Holly. I walked home deep in thought, almost surprised when I found myself at the side door. I climbed the stairs and put the pack in my room. That was when I remembered that I hadn't read the new protocol that Arson had sent me. I would have to do that later, it was time to work in the store.

I hustled down the stairs and into the back room to put the daily shipment away and file the packing slips. Ned stopped in while I was putting the last of it away.

"Got someone I'd like you to meet, he's coming over for supper tonight, so don't make any plans" and then he went back out front. Now I'll be wondering all afternoon just who this mysterious person could be.

We closed the store right at five as business had been slow anyway. I hadn't thought much about the break in at the farm with graduation being tomorrow afternoon. And don't forget the party! I was really excited about that; what a change in just four years. I had gone from living on a small survey ship to a school with over a hundred kids and teachers and getting to know all of these people. And, especially Ned and Henrietta, I'll never forget these two marvelous people.

I finished the paperwork and washed my hands before climbing the stairs to my room. It was almost supper time and Henrietta had gotten out the good china as she called it. But she had set the table for five people.

"Uh, Henrietta, Ned just said there was some guy coming for supper. Who is the other place for?"

"Ned hasn't heard, but our guest is bringing someone else along with him." She smiled at me and laughed. "Don't worry Jason" and she went back to stirring the stew.

At five minutes to five a car pulled up beside the store and a man and woman got out. I couldn't see who they were or recognize the car either.

"Jason, would you please escort our guests upstairs?" She asked.

I quickly descended the stairs and was surprised to see Mrs. Martin standing outside the door with her brother

Jerry. I was too shocked to say anything.

"You can close your mouth now young man" Jerry said with a smile, "I can see that Mrs. Johnson puts on a good feed just from looking at you."

"You sure have grown since we found you eating mice at the farm, Jason." Mrs. Martin said with a smile.

I could feel my face turning red from that comment; I'd learned so much since then.

"And I owe a lot of it to the two of you." I earnestly replied as we climbed up the stairs to the kitchen.

CHAPTER 28

There were introductions all around as Jerry had never met the Johnsons. Then we sat around the dining room table for a moment while Henrietta finished getting things together. I helped to serve and we made small talk during the meal.

Afterwards Henrietta and Mrs. Martin cleared the table while Ned led Jerry into the living room with me following. Jerry made some comments about how well they had done in taking care of me. Ned replied that they had really enjoyed the experience and were thankful that Mrs. Martin had brought me to them.

I sort of tuned it out as I remembered that I still hadn't read Arson's message as yet. I excused myself and said I'd be back in a moment. Inside my room I sat on the bed and read it through a couple of times somewhat puzzled over what he was telling me, it didn't quite go with what Arial had sent.

"Jason? We're all out here waiting on you; and bring

a chair too" Henrietta called.

"I'll be right there" I called back as I put the message back in my pack and hurried out to the living room. I had to get a chair from the kitchen to sit on. I hadn't realized how small our living room actually was until it was full of people, and there were only five of us!

"Jason" Ned began, "Mr. Sanders here has an interesting proposition for you."

"Let's take it a little slower than that" Jerry started. "First off, have you made any decision as to what you will be doing after graduation Jason?"

"Well, I'll be working here for the summer but I'm still torn about going on to college." I didn't want to make any commitments where I couldn't change plans quickly. I still wasn't sure when Dad and the rest would get back here. Arson's message was still fresh in my mind.

"Well, perhaps I can help you with that. I've spoken with Mr. Randall, your math teacher, and I think what I've got planned out will fit your needs perfectly. You don't mind going to Montana State University do you?"

"Are you saying that I should go to college?" I wasn't sure what he was getting at.

"I think that I can get you a full tuition scholarship in their special studies math program." He let that settle with me, but I could see from the look on his face that there was more to it, but Ned beat me to it.

"Seems to me to be quite a proposal you've offered

him, but why do I sense a big BUT attached to it?"

Jerry explained that it required a great amount of commitment on my part. I would be required to meet high moral and social standards and no less than a 3.8 grade point average; and even that would be subject to critique. He also explained that there were also some other contingencies such as Teaching Assistant duties as well.

I had a big decision to make and it had to be soon. I was faced with three possible avenues. What I most wanted was to stay right here and hope that they came for me soon. But that was overshadowed by the second possibility that if they didn't, I would have to join the military which, in itself, was a minimum three year commitment. Last option was to attend college which would get me deferred from having to join the military until after I finished college. There were some other methods to also being deferred, but I wasn't quite that desperate yet. Of course the option that Jerry offered me was quite enticing, a full Mathematics scholarship to Montana State University. And it's not like I had all summer to consider it either, Jerry had come up here special to make this offer. Of course he was staying with his family, but he wanted to have my answer before he went back on Sunday. That left me less than three days to make up my mind. And then, there was also graduation!

CHAPTER 29

Nothing I'd ever seen before matched the Pomp and Circumstance, or the speeches. We all had to dress up in black robes with funny hats that had a square board on top set off by a tassel that just wouldn't stay out of your face. And it was hot!

As second in our class's academic standing, I had earned the title of Salutatorian and it was my job to escort the Valedictorian to the podium; but at least I didn't have to give a speech. I figured that was the punishment for coming in second; and it suited me fine.

After the guests had taken their seats, the graduating class filed in and took their seats in the front two rows. Then the dignitaries filed in and took the stage all dressed in their robes, hats, and hoods; stopping in front of their chairs on the stage.

The clincher was when little Walter Webster stepped up beside the piano and played a short melody of some sorts on his trumpet; never did find out what it was called. But it sounded nice I guess, everyone clapped and then we all sat down.

The principal stepped forward and gave his speech and then introduced the superintendent, Mrs. Martin, who also gave a short speech. As superintendent, Mrs. Martin introduced the special guest, who of course was her brother Jerry. It was his pleasure, he stated, to introduce the Valedictorian, Holly Thatcher, who will be escorted by the Salutatorian, Jason Kingston. So much for remaining unnoticed!

The processional Marshall raised his baton, Walter blew a few more notes on his horn as Holly and I stood up together. We marched over to the stage. Just as we were about to climb the stairs, she turned around and whispered in my ear. I almost laughed out loud at what she told me.

"You needed that" she said as she winked at me and we climbed the stairs and marched over to the podium.

Then Holly gave her speech. I was quite impressed by what she had to say, she was very well poised and spoke with confidence. When she finished, she stepped back beside me and the Marshall started the procession with the rest of the first row. When the next classmate reached my side Jerry stepped back up to the podium to hand out the diplomas starting with Holly followed by the rest of us.

As we received our diplomas we shook hands with Jerry and then the rest of the dignitaries down to the other end of the stage, down the other set of stairs, and back to our seats.

"Was what you told me true?" I asked Holly as I sat down next to her and before Randall got there.

"Want to see?" as she leaned over next to me.

"Ah, no thanks, some things are better left to the imagination."

"I hear you're going to State also, what are you going to study there? I'm going into business?" She gave me a little pout.

"I'm not sure where you heard that, but it will probably be Math." Strange, it sounded like I had made up my mind.

"OH, big brainy thing are we now. You're going to need a shrewd business person to look after all those bright shiny inventions."

"I'll save the job interviews until I've got something worth selling." There were only a few more class mates left in line.

"I think you've got plenty to sell right now" she slyly winked at me as the last diploma was handed out and he descended the staircase and sat down at the end of the line. Walter then blew a few more notes that called us to attention and we all stood as Jerry paid his last sentiments to the class of '56. It was a neat little speech that I will always remember.

"Please be seated. This year we are starting something new." Jerry picked up a large envelope off the podium. "We have a few scholarships to award." He waited for the noise to quiet down.

"The first is to Randall Dressler for outstanding achievement." He waited until Randall had made his way back up to the podium.

"Four years ago he was barely passing Physical Ed" Jerry began. Then he had to wait a moment for the laughter to die down. Randall's face was beet red. "But with the help of his classmates, and the support of his friends and family, he has risen to third in the academic standings for his class. For that he has earned the Randwin Award." Jerry went on to explain about the award, they shook hands, and Randall made his way back to his seat.

I congratulated him as Jerry started to introduce the next award. "This award is from the Business College at Montana State University and is being presented to Holly Thatcher for her academic excellence."

Holly marched up to the podium with a big smile on her face. I thought that she was a little too smug about it, but what did I really care anyway. I congratulated her when she got back. She had taken her time posing for pictures all the way. I was a little appalled at her attitude. I pity the poor Joe that she finally traps into marriage.

"There remains one more award," and he waited for the clamor to die down again. He stood their calmly waiting for every ones attention. I think he really enjoyed giving them that dry hard look.

"This award has never been given to a student of Nashua High School before, and is not given at all unless the recipient has achieved high honors in both scholastic and social skills. Beyond that, the recipient must also be proposed as a candidate for this award by someone upon the board of directors of the university. That in itself is a rare thing and it has been several years since a suitable candidate has come before the board.

Four years ago I was asked to evaluate this individual as to their intelligence and ingenuity. This individual was faced with insurmountable odds both academically and socially coming from a completely different culture to live among us."

Somewhere along I started to get a strange feeling about who he was referring too.

"Therefore, as director of the department of admissions for Montana State University, it is with great pleasure that I now present this award to Jason Kingston, Nashua High School, Class of 1956."

The uproar was deafening, as I sat there in disbelief. Randall was pounding me on the back screaming at me. What do I do?

That was solved as Holly and Randall almost picked me up and escorted me to the stairs. They both hugged me and then I stumbled up the stairs and over to the podium.

I was still in shock when Jerry took my hand and softly spoke "Don't fall down on me yet son. Turn and face the audience, they want to take some pictures. I almost didn't notice the photographer facing us from in front of the stage.

Well, I guess that decision has been made for me. I wanted to crawl into a hole, but instead stood there as everyone was taking pictures. I don't remember leaving the stage, only that I made it back to my seat without tripping over my feet or falling down the stairs.

When I groggily awoke the next morning, I remembered going to the party, but the rest of the night was just a blur. There was a fleeting memory of a bonfire, dancing, loud music, and somewhere in the middle of all of it there was someone chasing a chicken. I have no idea what time it broke up or how I got home.

It was close to noon before I crawled out of bed to find Henrietta baking bread. I sat down at the table and she put a hot cup of coffee in front of me.

"Well, well. There is life after death isn't there?" She remarked.

Somehow I couldn't tell if she was chiding me or laughing at me; probably both.

CHAPTER 30

Ned and Henrietta were really proud of me and I was really appreciative of it. They had helped me with all of the paperwork and were with me when we went down to Billings to tour the campus and meet with some of the faculty. It was a quick trip over the weekend and back on Sunday. All that remained was filling out the last forms and getting dorm selections taken care of. It was still another month before school started; where had the summer gone?

I was lying on my bed rereading Arson's message again. I was trying to see if I could reconcile between the three messages. Dad's was straight forward, Arial's was disturbing, to say the least, and Arson's was mostly telling me what I was supposed to do between now and when they could get in touch with me again.

Wait a minute! How could I go off to college? I wouldn't be around in case they sent me a message? Could I remove the radio and take it with me? I had to find out.

I headed down the stairs and told Ned that I was going out to the farm, I shouldn't be too long. He waved to me from the front door as I rode my bike down the road. I was so wrapped up in my thoughts that I had forgotten about what had happened last spring. Just as I got to the driveway I glanced up toward the house before continuing on up to the next corner. I didn't see anything but decided to leave the bike in the bushes and sneak into the barn.

It was fortunate for me that the bushes were thick next to the window I used to get into the barn. I had started keeping all the barn doors locked from the inside. Once inside I rushed up the stairs and stole into the hidden flyer.

It seemed like an eternity before the flyers systems finally reached a ready state. I turned on the receiver and it immediately beeped once. Slowly I read through the contents. It had been received by the flyer nearly three weeks ago.

Jasom, we will be arriving at the derelict sight in two weeks. If things go well, we will park a satellite in orbit over you, close enough for the flyers broadcast to be able to reach it. Do not be surprised if it doesn't get answered immediately, we are not alone out here. For security reasons only broadcast on our own personal frequency.

Love, Mom and Dad.

I almost keyed the comm. and hollered out to them,

but as I sat there thinking about it, the contents of Arial's message came back to me. I needed to compose myself and think it through. Perhaps a quick summary of what I've done over the past four years and that I was going to attend college in the fall. Yes, that sounded about right.

I wrote it all down and recorded it then calmly keyed the broadcast to send it up to the satellite. How long should I wait, or should I? What did he mean they were not alone? Were the Queryl still around or did they have another ship accompany them? Or both?

Reluctantly I powered the flyer down and left the barn. On the ride back home I went over what he had told me. Darn it, I hadn't thought to look to see if I could remove the flyers radio. Next time I guess, had to come back again before I leave anyway.

I parked the bike in the garage and went up the stairs to the kitchen. Henrietta was stirring something on the stove.

"Jason, there was a call for you; the message is on your desk, something about school I think."

"Thanks" I told her and headed into my bedroom.

I didn't recognize the name, but the message was clear. Dorm assignments were in and I was going to be sharing a room with one of the Math TA's, some guy named Jared Wright, along with a phone number in case I had questions.

CHAPTER 31

I had been back out to the flyer, but there was no way to remove the radio. Besides I didn't have a portable power source and it would raise all sorts of questions if somebody found it. Sadly there was no message waiting either. I decided to not go back out there until the day before we were heading off to Billings. They would check me into school and spend the weekend with Ned's sister Becky and her family. It was their annual pilgrimage as they called it.

We found my dorm room and I started to put things away, there was no sign of my roommate yet. After we got all my stuff stored away Ned asked if I had enough money and Henrietta made me promise that'd I'd call them if I needed anything.

Over the last four years Ned had helped me to rent or lease out the farm fields that I'd inherited and the proceeds had gone into a bank. I had more than enough in there to pay the taxes and upkeep on the farm. I had transferred a modest amount of money over to a checking account in a local bank. I was now nineteen years old but Ned still had to cosign the account with me; I should be all set for the semester. They had planned to be back to pick me up at semesters end around thanksgiving and then again for Christmas. Winter semester would run until about mid-March, and then the spring semester would run until June.

I was lost in thought sitting there staring at the wall and didn't hear the person step into the room behind me.

"Hey space monkey get your boots on." the voice said in Wessar.

It took me by surprise as I hadn't heard my native language since I'd been here. Quietly I turned around to see who this person was. What I saw was a lanky red haired boy with a short scruffy beard.

"I beg your pardon" I replied in English.

"And here I thought you were Harkinson Kingston's son." He replied still speaking in Wessar. "But maybe I was mistaken" he continued in English, the foolish grin still in place.

"And whom might you be?" I asked, looking him over like he was a fish out of water.

"I'm your new bunky dude, names Jared Wright." we shook hands as he looked me over.

"Man you are so cool?" At least he was still speaking in English. "Where you from dude?"

"Dude?" I gave him a slightly disgusted look. "I'm

from Nashua."

"And what planet is Nashua on?" As he continued to grin at me.

"Nashua is a small farming community about 275 miles north of here." I gave him one more look over. "And just where are you from?" I tried to be as condescending as I could. My effort was wasted on him.

"Oh man, you won't like where I'm from, I'm Arial Haldon's cousin." He just tossed that into my lap and then disappeared down the hall. In a moment he was back with more stuff. "Dude! How about a hand with my stuff?"

Reluctantly I followed him out back to where his VW van was parked. The inside was filled with stuff. "You're not serious about bringing all this in are you? We don't have that much room" I complained.

"Naw, just this case and my typewriter." I took the case and left him the heavy looking machine.

Back upstairs, "Hey dude, looks like we're getting along real good here" as he stowed the typewriter under the bed.

I wasn't sure about that, he was almost as bad as Holly. I had a wicked thought, but no, I wouldn't set her on just anybody. Course if he got real bad I could introduce them.

"Oh man, I can see them wheels turning in your head, you've got some evil thoughts going on there dude." He grinned at me evilly. "Bet it has something to do with a girl?"

"Oh, nobody you'd be interested in, and I definitely don't think she'd care for you either."

He dropped the dudeness for a moment and switched back to Wessar "First commandment when living amongst the natives, stay away from the women."

"That's for sure" I replied bleakly. I didn't realize that I used Wessar to answer him.

"You sure are good, Harkinson and Valya didn't raise no fool." then the façade slipped back in place. "Hey dude, your parents have any kids that lived?"

He wasn't laughing alone, two upper classman by the looks were lurking in the doorway leering at me. I leered right back at them. One of them blinked before I did and I let a sly smile creep onto my face. They both turned a little pale.

"Hey guys, like you to meet an old buddy from back where I come from. He likes my cousin but she's just teasing him along so go easy on him or he might tear your head off."

They had stopped laughing by then.

CHAPTER 32

I wasn't sure how much I could trust Jared. On the one hand he spoke Wessar and was related to Arial. But, on the other hand, what was he doing here? By the looks he may have been here longer than I had. What should I do?

I did what anyone in this situation would do, I procrastinated. I stuck with English, less chance of slipping up. When we were alone I fished for information when I could.

"So Jasom, what is Nashua like?" I was deep in History homework.

"Well, dude" a little caricature of him, "How much of this state do you know?" I quizzed him. "You've been here how long now, and you've never heard of Nashua?"

"I've spent most of my time right here in Billings. We were let down in the mountains about a hundred miles west of here. Mission is to spend a few years building a solid background before moving into the mainstream economy."

We sparred back and forth through that semester. But it was good to have someone to help with some of my homework especially one who has spent more time in the college system. This was not high school, and the politics of college life were definitely more cut throat than a public school.

It was the last day of the semester and I was packing a few things to take home with me. Ned and Henrietta were going to pick me up in a couple of hours outside the dorm.

"Hey dude" Jared called as he slipped in the door. "Your ride's here. They're natives aren't they?"

"I thought you knew that?" I didn't quite like his tone of voice.

"Hey. No offense man." And he picked up his bags and headed out the door. "See ya, dude." and he was gone.

CHAPTER 33

The ride back home was strange. I remembered the scenery, memorized it the first trip down three years ago. Not much had changed since then, but I felt different. Henrietta chattered almost continuously the first hundred miles and I answered what I could. That was before I fell asleep. I drifted in and out for a while until we got to the Fort Peck Dam.

As I came fully awake, Henrietta was telling Ned how to drive. That in itself was amusing, they hadn't changed much.

"So, what have you two been up to while I've been slaving away in school?"

"It's been kind of quiet around the house" Ned chuckled, "she wants to get a dog to take your place. Other than that, the crops this year did quite well, and all of the fields have been rented for next year. Are you going to need some more money for next semester?"

"Probably, but we can go over the figures later, I

The Orphan from Space

just want to unwind for a while."

"Farms still standing and no sign of anymore break ins. Trouble is, an unused house will stand for a long time, but being closed up it's going to smell terrible. It will go a few years like that and then it will start to rot from the inside out."

I was a little alarmed by that. "What can we do for it then?"

"I was thinking you should rent it out. Have someone living there, someone to care for it, you know what I mean?" Ned asked.

"I do, but I don't know if I could trust just anyone. You have someone in mind?" I inquired.

"Actually I do" Ned replied. "Thought some about moving out there, just the two of us, but it wouldn't be as easy to take care of the store and we'd just feel so all alone in that big house."

"So?" I prodded.

"Well" he started, "there's this young family in town that's got a small cottage just down the street from the store. It's a might bigger than what we have now, and we could rent out the space above the store as an apartment."

"And those stairs are beginning to wear us out" Henrietta remarked.

"So you're proposing that I rent the house to them, you'll buy their cottage and rent the upstairs above the store?" I thought about it. I was a little leery about the flyer

161

hidden in the barn. Was there somewhere else I could keep it?

"I like the idea, and of course have some misgivings. There is a lot of personal stuff I've got stored in the barn and in the attic that may have to move somewhere else though." Or should I just put better locks on the doors and make the flyers hideout a little more secure. I could try that for a while and if it doesn't work out, move it later.

"We should go over and talk to them first" Ned continued, "then we can make some better plans."

By then we had pulled into the driveway beside the store. The sun was just setting behind the mountains to the west and it was getting colder by the minute. Almost felt like there was a storm coming. I shivered and started hauling my stuff up to my room. I could see by the way Henrietta climbed the stairs that it was beginning to wear her out. I didn't say anything about it. I was just glad that we'd stopped at a restaurant in Brockway for supper, Henrietta looked beat.

CHAPTER 34

The next morning I was up early and went down to meet the first truck of the week. I put away the shipment, filed the paperwork, and restocked the shelves. I heard the tinkle of the front door bell as the first customers of the morning came in. I washed off my hands in the back sink and went out to help Ned.

"Well, well, look who's back" I heard Mrs. Thatcher say. "How was life at the big university?"

"Not too bad, and definitely not what I thought it would be. Life is surely strange around that place."

"That's the same thing that Holly said in her last letter. I hope she's doing well."

"Isn't she coming home over the break?" I asked.

"Yes, but the bus doesn't get in until later this afternoon. When did you get back?"

"We picked him up yesterday afternoon" Ned told her, "didn't get back here till after ten last night."

"I would have asked her to ride with us if I'd

known." I was trying to be kind but wasn't sure Either Ned or Henrietta would have gone along with that idea. Some people might have gotten the wrong idea.

"Oh, don't worry about that, I wouldn't have let her impose on you." She gave me a wink and an understanding look. "But I appreciate the offer. If it came down to necessity I would hope the offer would still be open?"

"Of course Mrs. Thatcher" Ned told her, "just let me know and it would be no problem at all."

"Thank you" she replied as I picked up her bags and carried them to her car. "I'll tell her you said hello."

I smiled at her and she drove off. Hadn't really thought much about Holly, or seen her either. The university had several colleges and the business college was on the other side of campus, and apparently we didn't have any classes together. Oh well, I had other things to worry about.

"Jason, I'm expecting another truck about lunch time, this one is a special delivery from Montgomery Ward in Chicago. It's a small shipment so I'll handle it." He said goodbye to the Wilburs and sat down on the counter behind the cash register as they left the store. He had been setting there for so many years that the front edge of the shelf was completely worn down where he rested his feet.

"Given any more thought to renting out the farm?" he asked.

"I can see that the farm house needs to be lived in

but I don't want to sell it. You can vouch for them? Ah, what does he do for a living and how big a family do they have?"

"I'll vouch for them, already talked to them about it too. They have three little ones, I think the oldest is just starting school. Besides Henrietta likes their little cottage. It has three bedrooms instead of our little two."

He scratched the back of his neck, must be a new shirt, he always tears the tag off the new ones. "When can I meet them? I've only got a couple of weeks before school starts. If they're going to be moving out there I'll have to get my stuff out or stored somewhere else." I fidgeted for a moment while Ned sat back lost in thought.

"Can you do without me for a while, I should run out there and get a look at just how much stuff I'll have to put in storage." I had another reason for the trip, but he didn't need to know about that one.

"Heh, just what do you think I've been doing for the last three months without you?" He watched out the front window as a car pulled into the yard. "Go ahead, I'll do fine. Just be back before five, there's a weather front coming in and there might be rain."

I went out the back to the garage and took my bike off the rack. The tires were a little soft so I filled them up and tried it out in the yard before heading down the road to the turn out to the farm. About part way out I felt a cool breeze and was glad I had brought a wool jacket.

CHAPTER 35

I climbed through the barn window and went up the stairs. At the top of the stairs I quietly opened the door after listening for any noises. I was letting things from the past catch up with me, but there hadn't been any problems out here since that incident about a year ago. Funny thing, Hiram had never let us know exactly what had happened with the investigation.

I slipped through the secret doorway and into the flyer. A minute can seem like an eternity as I waited for the systems to come on line. There were three beeps this time. Finally, some answers.

The first was again from Arson about protocols; that one could wait. The next was from mom. I eagerly read through it twice, the second time to make sure I understood what she had meant by 'shared discovery'.

Mom's message gave details on how they were coming with accessing the derelict. They had managed to sell the return expedition to the council, but the council had added a second ship with a company of scientists. This was to be what they called a 'shared discovery' mission.

Jasom,

Their first effort was to move all of the asteroids in the vicinity far away from it so that they could examine the hull and gain access to the interior. The Tarkna is the name of the other ship. At first they moved several asteroids out of the way but not far enough as they were pulled back in by some invisible force. Finally they would pull one out and then force it well beyond the influence of the ships invisible force field. This is taking a lot of time, but they are slowly isolating it.

In the meantime they have dropped a probe into the area around it and remapped its exterior surface. As best they could determine from the outlines and hatch placements, this is a much newer ship then any of the other ones that had been found so far. They have also determined, from these views, which one is the main entrance and they are concentrating their efforts on opening up that hatch. What is most surprising is that the ship is apparently under power just as we thought when we found it. It is my considered opinion that the ship is waiting for something or someone to return to it. I have other theories as well which I have discussed with the rest of our crew, but for now we're keeping them to ourselves.

From what your father and I can determine, the only reason we were allowed on this expedition was that we wouldn't tell them where it was unless they did. Many of the personnel on the other ship are associated with a new radical political party on the council. We are worried what will happen if they find they no longer need us.

Jasom, please realize that you're not alone. I have discovered that Arson's estranged relative and his family, whom he hasn't heard from in many years, are living somewhere near you. Be careful around them as they have grand plans to form their own empire and apparently starting with this planet. I don't think that they know about the derelict yet. Again, I advise extreme caution.

Love, Mom, Dad and Dora

I slowly read it a third time before printing it out along with Arson's protocol. I'd read his later tonight.

The last one was again from Arial. What surprised me the most was that she was actually sending me a message. I'd had a crush on her since I was nine. Back then she had been thirteen and I was beneath her notice. Again, it seemed that things have changed.

Jasom,

I am attaching this message to Dad's so that no one else knows that I'm sending this to you. I don't think he knows I'm doing this but it's necessary for you to hear my views on what *is going on.*

Many things have changed. I was old enough to attend the council meetings and listened with disgust at the way they were handled. The fools first said that we should leave these things alone; they would bring no good in the end. Those stupid fools should be put out of their misery instead of letting them sit in positions of power. They called themselves conservatives, but I would have called them something a lot worse.

In the end it wasn't the conservatives or the progressives that won out. There truly is a mix of viewpoints on the council, but the majority, were in our favor. It was a hard fought win and not without concessions on all sides. That's how we got saddled with all these idiotic scientists.

I don't mind scientists Jasom, but the ones that I've met on this expedition aren't very open to views outside the accepted norm. Most of them don't even believe what we found actually exists. I guess they're in for a shock.

I have some other bad news and I hope it reaches you before it's too late. My cousin Jared may be somewhere near you, be very wary of him. I've never met him but from what I've heard he is a strange child. His parents are worse, dreams of grandeur and global sabotage would be my guess.

Your friend forever, Arial

Should I send an answer back now? I checked the receipt date and time; I had just missed them by a day.

I decided to wait; I needed to think about what was safe to tell them. There was the possibility that these transmissions were being intercepted, I would have to choose my wording carefully.

Strange, there was no mention of the Queryl either. I should ask about that.

I checked my watch, it was getting late and I still hadn't gone through the house yet. I folded the printouts as the flyer powered down and sadly locked the hatch.

I went through the house, from the attic down to the cellar, and about the only things worth saving were the Hooch and some of the clothing that still fit me. The kitchen utensils and bedding I'd have to ask Ned and Henrietta about as well as the rest of the clothing.

I locked the house up and rode down the driveway to the road. I was glad I'd brought my jacket as it was starting to get really cold. I quick glance to the west and I started to hurry, it didn't look like rain coming, more like a blizzard.

I was hanging the bike in the garage when the snow began to fall. It was heavy and wet and promised more than a few inches if it kept up all night. I stepped out of the garage and was just closing the doors when I heard a voice from across the road calling to me.

"Hey! Jason!" I turned and saw Hiram Wheeler motioning for me to come over.

I hollered back to him that I would be over in just a

minute and rushed up the stairs to tell Henrietta that I was back and that Hiram Wheeler wanted to talk to me.

"Just don't be too long Jason, supper's almost ready. If you want you can ask him if he'd like to join us, there's enough for four of us." She was being generous; she really didn't care much for Mr. Wheeler.

I slogged through the falling snow over to the door he held open for me. I brushed off the snow and followed him into his office.

"When did you get back? Didn't expect you until tomorrow when the bus gets here."

"Ned and Henrietta came down and picked me up as soon as I was finished, got back late last night. I thought the bus came today though, Holly is supposed to be on it?"

"The old grey dog broke down in Brockway yesterday afternoon. All the passengers had to spend the night in the bus depot" he chuckled. "Boy you lucked out, in more ways than one." He gave me that mischievous look that told me that he knew all about my dealings with Holly Thatcher.

"You know that she takes after her mother?" he added with a sly grin.

"Is that what you wanted to talk to me about?" Didn't need to go down that road. "And Henrietta says you can come over for supper if you'd like."

That surprised him. "Really now?" He paused in thought, "That is an offer I won't refuse. Let me get my coat and a flashlight."

He turned off the lights and locked his door and we trudged across the road and up the stairs. He was huffing a little when we got to the kitchen door. I opened the door and let him into the kitchen. Henrietta was stirring something on the stove and gave him an odd smile.

"Thought that would get you out of that old house of yours. When's the last time you had a good meal Hiram?"

"It's been many a year and I appreciate the offer, as does Mildred."

"Yes" she replied, "I miss her dearly too. Go ahead sit down at the table, Ned will be right up, I sent him after the last jar of preserves."

Hiram and I sat at the table making idle conversation about my first semester at the university. I hadn't known that he was also a graduate from the university as was his late wife Mildred. Strange to think that I was going to the same school that he had gone too.

"Well, it took you long enough." Henrietta was scolding Ned as he brought up the jar from the store room.

"Reminded me of something I hadn't done yet so I took care of that first. Nice of you to join us Hiram, it's been a long time since the last time we got together. Anything new to report?" Ned asked, prodding him for an update on the investigation.

"Why don't we save that for after supper, it's been

some time since I've had a meal I haven't made myself. I intend to enjoy it" as he gladly filled his plate.

We gathered in the living room afterwards and Hiram asked how school was going. I told them it was a different experience and that I'd met a lot of new people and made some new friends.

"Well that's nice" he replied, "but in particular I was wondering if you had run into a student by the name of Harold Cross. I had heard that he was in the same area of study that you were pursuing."

"I've may have heard the name, and we might even be in the same class, but it's hard to say, most of my classes have at least thirty students in them. What does he look like?"

"He's a year of two older than you, red curly hair and a hippie attitude, calls everyone he knows dude."

I carefully avoided looking at him while I asked, "What is your interest in him, should I avoid him?"

"Well the reason I asked is that I've heard some rather disturbing things about this person. And he might even be part of the group that broke into your farm house."

"The only names I remember from back then were chief and Hawthorne. Find out anything more about them?"

"Well, Jason, Hawthorne was picked up last month trying to burglarize a house on the outskirts of Billings. It will be quite a while before he's back on the streets. And while they were questioning him they found out who chief was. He's already behind bars for trying to hold up a bank in Wyoming. That last part is disturbing though, it's a long way from here down to Laramie. I'm thinking that his partner in the robbery was the third guy in your burglary case. And that means that all three of them are in custody and will be doing time for a few years." He closed his eyes and smiled. "Nothing like a good meal to make me feel sleepy." He stood up and stretched, "I should be going before the snow gets to deep."

I walked him down to the back door.

"There was one other thing Jason" he said with his hand on the door knob, "I noticed you wince when I described him. You've met him as well I'd guess. What name is he going under now?"

I decided it best to tell what I knew without letting on to his real background.

"He goes by the name of Jared Wright; he's a third year student, and my roommate." I watched his face closely for any signs of what he was thinking.

"Well, best I can suggest is to be wary. Don't get too involved in any outside activities with him or any of his buddies. It might not turn out to well for you. Here" he passed me a business card, "this is the name of the local trooper in the Billings area. He's undercover so just use your name and he'll know how to help you get in touch with me."

"I knew I should have brought my boots." With that he said good night and headed home through the falling snow.

CHAPTER 36

We met with the young family from down the street the following day after he got home from work. Ted and Martha Farnham had three young children, with the oldest starting first grade in the fall. The small cottage just didn't have the room they would need as the children grew older. He had a steady well-paying job working as the head mechanic at the local farm supply store and his wife did something with mail ordering from home. She was also expecting their fourth child in the spring.

We settled on an agreeable monthly rent and we also advised them on keeping the children out of the fields as there would be machinery moving about during the summer months. I explained that I hadn't had time to move all of my stuff out of the upstairs but would try to get it taken care of before I went back to school. Some parts of the house, such as the cellar, attic, and barn would be off limits. I also informed them that we would leave all of the furniture for their use and we would also close off the back addition. It was empty, and they would be allowed to store things out there but it was unheated.

If they needed anything they should call Ned. He would collect the rent as he did with all of the rental fields, and I would show up from time to time when I was in the area to see how things were going.

All things considered I thought it would work out well. The rental cottage they had been living in was owned by Hiram Wheeler next door. He gladly took Ned's offer for the cottage as he was thinking of moving to Billings. That meant that both houses were up for sale.

Ned and I talked it over and as Hiram's place was the larger dwelling, he bought that one and helped me to purchase the cottage using the farm as collateral. With any luck he could rent out the upper floor of the store and I could get a tenant for the cottage; I couldn't have done it without Ned and Henrietta, they were so good to me.

CHAPTER 37

I spent most of the next two weeks cleaning out the farm house and moving stuff into the barn. I converted the tack room into a place where everything I wanted to keep separate could be stored. Most of it was in trunks that I found in the attic. While I was at it I rebuilt the wall that hid the flyer and put in a secret entry from the tack room which in turn was disguised with a bed frame leaned in front of it.

I also took the time to send a well composed message to both Arson and Mom. I saw how Arial had tagged her message along with her fathers as a hidden attachment, and I did the same with my reply to her.

In my message to mom, I had told her that I missed them terribly but had been taken in by a kindly couple who didn't have any children. The farm was doing well, most of the fields have been rented out to local farmers and the house to a nice young couple with three and a half kids. I'm sure she'd understand the implication. I let her know that it would be several weeks before I could communicate with them again.

My message to Arial was mostly the same but I mentioned my roommate reminded me of her and described Jared as best I could. I didn't say anything about him to mom because I was afraid she'd worry. I just sent a short message to Arson saying that I understood and really wished it were possible for me to be there with them.

I sat in the control chair for nearly five minutes after sending them off. I really wished that I could be out there with them exploring the derelict. By the sounds, it would be nearly three years before they would make much more progress. But things go on, and I should be heading back home. I checked on the Hooch, and picked up four more pints for Ned to use as he saw fit; not enough for him to get into trouble over. I was sure that Henrietta knew about it, but she didn't say anything. I had also discovered that the two pints I had set aside had disappeared around graduation time. We must have had some party that night.

I locked up the barn and checked the house once more before driving back to the store. I've been here just over four years, and if things go well, before long I would be a land lord with a fairly stable income. I parked the car in the garage and bounced up the stairs. Henrietta was in the kitchen as usual and Ned was in the living room reading the paper.

"It's been nice having you around for a few days" Ned said looking up from the paper. "We didn't realize just how lonely we'd been until you came into our lives."

"I miss you guys too. Sometimes it gets lonely in the dorm even with so many people around."

"How you getting along with your room mate dear?" Henrietta asked.

"Oh, he's OK I guess, but he'll be moving on before long. Next year he'll be a senior and moving off campus with the rest of his pals." I sat down on the couch and stared at the ceiling. "You still haven't fixed the hole in the ceiling have you?"

"Heh, heh, you noticed. I'll get to that soon enough; have to do it before the new tenants move in."

"Have you found someone yet?" I asked.

"Don't let him fool you Jason, he hasn't even advertised yet. Besides" she said, "we still have to clean out Hiram's place and he won't be moving for another week yet."

"Sometimes I wish I didn't have to go back to college…" I mused.

"Then remember what the alternatives are" Henrietta reminded me. "Don't worry son, you're doing the right thing. You'll be done school before you know it."

Considering all aspects of my situation I guess things are going OK, but I still wish I knew what was going on with mom and dad. I was happy that they were close by, but my elation was short lived as I thought through the consequences of being reunited with my real family. I thought about Mom, Dad, and my little sister, the twerp. I missed them terribly but it had been so long, almost a life-time ago. On one hand, I couldn't wait to see them again. On the other hand, it would mean leaving all of my friends behind; especially Ned and Henrietta.

"Something bothering you, son?" Ned asked. "You're looking awful glum."

I took a deep breath and thought of happier things, like what was for supper; absolutely nothing could beat Henrietta's cooking. "No, just thinking about things that I can't do anything about."

"Welcome to the world of adults" Ned chuckled. "If you can't do anything about it why are you worried about it? Things have a way of working out, sometimes in the strangest ways." Ned folded the paper in his lap, "Mrs. Thatcher called while you were gone. She was wondering if we could give Holly a ride back to college. Is that alright with you?" he asked.

"Fine with me, it's your car. I think I can put up with her for that long." Then I burst out laughing, "If things get to bad in the back seat, just pull over to the side of the road and put me out of my misery."

"Jason! Is that anyway to talk?" Henrietta squawked as Ned was laughing with me.

"Henrietta, have you ever met Holly?"

"I'll have you know that I stole Ned away from her mother." She had a look of embarrassment on her face, "I've heard she's just like her mother too."

My, what you learn about your parents can sometimes be really shocking. "I think that Holly and I have reached a mutual understanding along those lines. Simply stated" I mimicked, "Thou shalt not get involved."

They both laughed at that.

CHAPTER 38

We survived the trip back to college, Holly was on her best behavior and I noticed that she'd slimmed down a lot more. Probably had to with the high heels she was wearing. We dropped her off at her dorm and then left me at mine. It was early and Jared wasn't back yet so we walked around the campus for a while before saying good bye. Tonight they were staying with Ned's sister before heading back early in the morning.

I had checked the flyer for replies, but there hadn't been any. Maybe I could wheedle more information out of Jared when he gets in. Sometimes I can catch him at the right moment and he'll say more then he thinks. It was hard living with him because he seemed starved to speak with someone of his own kind. So far I've found that type of thinking to be elitist. That's why I had to be careful with him.

For some odd reason Jared didn't show up that evening, or the next day either. I had collected my books and started attending classes by then and hadn't really missed him until someone showed up from the main office.

"Is this Jared Wright's room?"

Without looking up I replied, "Depends on whose asking?" I had been caught once by that routine before.

"And you are who?" the stranger asked.

"Depends on who's asking?" I was beginning to get tired of this.

"Do you know who you're talking too?" he demanded.

"No, and if you don't prove who you are, you're going to learn how the Wright brothers felt." a slight pause for effect, "Without the plane."

"Young man, I'm Doctor Arnold Stein, Dean of the Engineering College, Special Studies."

He did bear some semblance to the only picture I've ever seen of him.

"So you're not one of Jared's cronies trying to pull another stupid stunt on me?" might as well make myself look like the victim here.

That softened his expression a little.

"I would suggest that in the future you be more careful how you speak to members of the faculty young man."

"And how would I know who they are unless they identify themselves" I replied exasperatedly. "I've been taken in by several schemes with people telling me they are someone they're not."

"Perhaps I should have informed you of who I was first" he replied reluctantly.

"Thank you, sir. And I'll remember what you told me as well. You are looking for Jared Wright? I haven't seen him since the end of last semester." I waved around at the clutter on the other side of the room. "But most of his stuff is still here so I would assume that he will be coming back."

"I'm not so sure about that. I thought you two were from the same place?"

"Why would you think that?" I asked.

"Several of your class mates say you both speak the same foreign language. I'd assumed that you were close."

"Sorry sir, I had never met him until last fall. And yes I do know his cousin quite well, but not him." That should cover everything that we had said.

"Very well then, I'll get someone to clean out his things and put them in storage."

"He's not coming back to school then?" I didn't like the sound of this.

"What little I've heard is that he has transferred back east to another college nearer his family."

He was fishing for information, but I just shrugged my shoulders. "I can pack his stuff up, most of its still in the boxes he brought it in. I would hate to have some of my stuff get packed by mistake." I had the legitimate concern.

"Very well then, I'll have the custodial staff bring a

cart up for it."

With that he left. I had some other questions, but didn't want to appear too interested; after all, I really didn't know him that well. I quickly thought over what studies I had to do and decided to do the packing right now. Maybe I could find something interesting.

An hour later I had most of it taken care of. He had taken all of his clothes when he left. I found nothing of interest in any of the boxes under the bed except for the typewriter. I slid it out onto the floor and opened the top and admired the primitive engineering that would eventually lead to computer keyboards sometime in the future.

I put the typewriter on the desk after stacking all of his boxes in the center of the room. Then I gathered all the trash in the basket and headed out back to the dumpster. Most of the students just left it for the janitorial services but I was taught to keep my own space clean and clutter free.

Out the back door, down the steps, and across the lawn to a cross walkway, then down by the parking lot, lift the cover and empty the contents of the waste basket into the dumpster.

I closed the cover on the dumpster and walked back up the sidewalk beside the parking lot. I was facing the sun wondering what tomorrows weather would bring when I happened to notice Jared's VW van parked in the same spot it had been that first day when I helped him haul his stuff into the dorm.

I walked over and peered in the windows, looked just as messy as ever. Then I glanced at the parking sticker, it had expired at the end of last semester. The college didn't miss a trick on charging for things, you had to pay in advance just to park in their lots for a semester. I tried the door and was amazed to find it was unlocked. Either Jared was trusting or there was nothing in it worth stealing.

Sitting on the dash was a piece of paper with my name on it. After a moment I realized that it was written in Wessar, it was also meant for me to find it. I opened it up and read.

Jasom,

Hey there dude! In case I don't see you before I leave I want you to have my van. The keys are in my stuff in the room along with the bill of sale transferring ownership over to you. I would strongly suggest that you either move it off campus or pay for a parking permit before they haul it away. I know it's not worth much, but consider it a friendly token from me to you. Until we meet again dude.

Jared

I put the note in my pocket wondering what I should do. A car would be helpful, but I didn't have the keys or the bill of sale in hand. Frantically I ran back into the dorm hoping they hadn't hauled away the boxes I had left outside the room.

At the top of the stairs I saw a custodian with a cart coming from my room. "Hey there" I hollered, "wait up a moment!"

I quickly told him what I needed and he waited while I dove into the box containing the papers. Fortunately they were right on top. "I thanked him for his patience and headed down to the admissions office. They sent me down the hall to the security office where I got all of the paperwork taken care of and decided to buy the sticker. The girl at the desk also told me that I had thirty days to notify the motor vehicles department and have the tags changed.

From there it was back to the parking lot. I got the sticker in place just as the security patrol was coming through.

"What are you up to there, son?" the burly officer asked me.

"Just bought this old van from one of the departing seniors and had to get the sticker updated. Next is cleaning it out." I made a disgusted look.

"I doubt if there are any treasures in that old clunker, have you checked to make sure it runs?" With that he continued his rounds and left.

Hadn't thought of that. With great amount of dread I climbed in behind the wheel and turned the key. With a great sigh of relief I listened to the engine start and run smoothly. Probably should also give it a road test.

It was well after dark when I finally had the interior cleaned out. Next time out I'd take it to a car wash. I locked the doors and headed up to my room. I still had some studying to do. I pushed on my door, but it wouldn't open, it was locked. I don't remember locking it, but then again maybe the custodian had locked it after I ran off to get the van taken care of.

I unlocked my door and flipped on the light switch as I walked in. I heard the door click shut behind me, but I couldn't believe what I was seeing in front of me.

CHAPTER 39

It was if time stood still for me in that moment. Facing me with a fearful look on her face was Arial. I couldn't believe my eyes. She hadn't changed a bit and seemed a little shorter than I remembered.

"Jasom, is that you?" There was no mistaking the quaver in her voice, and that was something that I had never expected from her. To me she was the dashing red headed pilot that I had loved from afar for so long.

"You look so different!" There was no doubt of her fear.

"Arial why...how...what are you doing here? It's been almost five years...is there something wrong?"

Suddenly she did the one thing I would never have suspected, she leaped across the room and wrapped her arms around me and started sobbing on my shoulder. Gently I held her until she calmed down.

"Arial, how did you get here and how on earth did you find me?"

"Jasom, you look so different and you sound so different. Oh there's so much to tell you and we don't have much time, Dora and Tomer…"

"You have Dora and Tomer with you?" This was beginning to sound real bad. "Where are they?"

"They're hiding in the bushes outside, it would look funny to bring them into a place like this; someone might ask the wrong questions."

"Yes I know, and you'd have to hurt them. I know all about it."

I thought fast. There was nowhere around here that I could take them unless we went to one of the motel's that cater to the tourists. Again, there might be too many questions asked there as well.

"OK, this is what we're going to have to do. There is only one place I know of that's safe and it will take several hours to reach it. I need to make an excuse for leaving."

She sat quietly on my bed while I gathered all of my clothes and valuables and hurriedly wrote a note for the office. I grabbed her hand and headed toward the door.

"Come with me" I commanded as we headed down the stairs to the back door. Out in the parking lot I unlocked the van and tossed my bag inside. "Go get the kids and meet me back here, I'll only be a minute." I rushed down to the office hoping someone would still be there.

Luckily Mrs. Stillwell was still at her desk and just beginning to get ready to leave. I'd met her the first day here. She had personally helped me find where everything was and told Henrietta and Ned that she'd look after me.

"Why Jason, how are you doing?" she smiled at me. "I was just headed home, is there something I can do for you?"

I told her that I had a family emergency and had to leave immediately. I gave her the note which only gave my contact number at home and little else.

"That's not much of an excuse." she told me. "Please let me know all you can as soon as you can, promise?"

"Yes, Mrs. Stillwell; and I really appreciate all you've done for me. Hopefully I can get this issue resolved quickly." I gave her a quick smile and ran back to the car.

When I got back to the car it was dark and I couldn't see anyone around.

"Arial?" I said in a low voice. "Are you here?"

Three heads popped up in the windows. Little Dora's eyes were wide open with awe. "Jasom!" she screamed and jumped out of the door and wrapped her arms around my middle. How did she get to be so short? Tomer just sat on the back seat and stared at me as if he didn't know me. After a moment she looked up at me.

"Jasom, how did you get so big?" It dawned on me what had happened, but explanations would have to wait.

"Back in the van everyone, we're leaving here now." I started the engine and pulled out of the parking lot and down the lane to the street. I had watched Ned drive this way and was pretty sure I could find my way over to 87 North. Once on the way, Arial started filling me in on why they were here.

Disaster had happened; mom and dad were imprisoned by the crew from the other ship, and Tomer's parents had been killed for no apparent reason. Arson had made a quick decision and had taken Arial, Dora, and Tomer and brought them to just outside Billings where he knew some local people. They had been given proper clothing and then brought to the campus. Arson had then headed back to try and save the others.

Fortunately little Selda hadn't been with them on this trip, she was staying back home with relatives and attending school. Now poor Tomer was an orphan and if things didn't work out, that would be the fate of the rest of us.

"I'm hungry." Tomer complained from the back. He was sitting in the middle next to Dora who was trying to comfort him.

"When did you eat last?" I asked Arial.

"Honestly I don't remember; it seems like hours ago." I heard another stomach growl.

"I know a place not far from here. We'll stop and get something to eat there. It's not too much further up to Roundup; we should be there in another ten minutes or so." Bailey's Diner was a small family run diner right on the highway; a place where a lot of the truckers stopped. The place didn't look like much, but the food was good.

There were hardly any cars or trucks parked outside when I pulled up to the front row and our bedraggled crew walked in and sat down in a corner booth. I ordered for everyone and took Tomer to the bathroom. When we got back the food hadn't come yet so I showed Arial where to go and Dora went with her. Hopefully she could figure out the plumbing.

They both looked in better spirits when they came back. I sat on the outside with Dora beside me. "How are you doing twerp" hoping the old familiarity would help her calm down.

"I'll survive I guess. Did you get our messages?" She sounded a little better, but it would take some time with Tomer. Arial was doing what she could with him. He was just calming down when the food arrived. I wasn't sure how much he would eat in his bedraggled condition, but he sat there and mechanically ate most of it. About then I noticed his eyes beginning to droop. I saw Arial smile at him as he leaned against her half asleep.

"Hurry up and finish, we've still got a few more hours to go." I checked the time, it was late, we weren't going to get there before ten unless we hurried and I still haven't called Henrietta yet. Seems like it had been one rush since I'd walked into my room only what, two hours ago.

"Arial? Take them out to the van I have to make a

phone call." She nodded and waited for Dora to finish her hot dog and scoop up the french fries covered with ketchup. I could hear her slurping the last of her soda as I was putting money in the phone.

Ned answered the phone. When he heard my voice he panicked. "Jason? What's wrong? Is it serious? Do we need to come get you?" then I heard another voice in the background.

"Hello? Jason, is that you?" Henrietta asked. "Ned is having a fit. Tell me what's wrong."

"First tell him to calm down there's nothing wrong with me, I just bought a car and I've a family problem that I need help with?"

"Family problem?" she asked suspiciously.

"No, Henrietta, not that kind of family problem. I need to… correction, I'm on my way home and I'm bringing some of my family with me. I don't have time to explain, we're just leaving Roundup now and should be getting there about ten. There will be four of us, is it all right if we stay with you?"

"Now that's nothing you need to ask, you're always welcome and we'll find a place for everyone when you get here. Oh, and what ages?"

"My time is almost up, 8, 10, and 19" just as the connection died.

CHAPTER 40

It was just over an hour to the last turn north up to Fort Peck dam. Dora and Tomer had fallen asleep not long after we left the restaurant. I noticed that Arial was half asleep for a while until I headed north off 200. I heard a yawn and glanced over to see her stretching.

"Where did you get this ugly vehicle?" she asked. "It smells bad, sniff, really bad."

"I just bought it this afternoon from your cousin Jared."

"You what?!" Whoa, I have never seen her that shocked before.

"Yeah, he left me a note saying he'd signed owner-ship over to me; I got the papers and all. The dean stopped by and told me he was going back east somewhere so I boxed his things up for him."

"I wonder what they're doing here? They were ban-ished from Renland years ago, probably nothing good." She didn't have much love for that part of the family I guess.

I remembered where Renland was, a small star cluster just a few light-years from Evenset where my family was from.

"What were they banished for? I've never heard you mention them before."

"That's something even I don't know about, no one in the family will discuss it so it must have been something really messy. That's all I know."

"Something has me puzzled though, how come Dora and Tomer don't look any bigger than when I last saw them?"

"You've forgotten that we go into cold sleep when the engines are running full speed. That's the only way we could outrun the Queryl. We're only a few months older then when they left you here." She gave me a quizzical look. "Just how long have you been here?"

"I thought as much." I did the math in my head. "I've been here just long enough to be older than you are by about three months, if I remember your birthday correctly."

"You've been here that long? I had no idea" she replied sadly.

"It hasn't been that bad" and I told her how they had found me eating mice and preserves and placed me with this nice couple which was where we were going.

I told her about high school, the teachers, Mrs. Martin and the others, and for some odd reason I also told her about Holly.

She was strangely quiet the rest of the way.

It was just a little past ten when I pulled in beside the garage and turned off the engine. I knew they were up and waiting for us as the upstairs lights were on and the stairway light came on just as I was lifting Dora out of the back seat.

I turned around and Ned was standing there, Arial was in the back seat trying to pick Tomer up.

"You have any luggage Jason?" he asked.

"Just the bag on the floor in the back. Could you get the door and we'll carry these sleepy heads upstairs."

It was a struggle hauling Dora up those stairs; she was heavier than I remembered. Upstairs I introduced Arial and told them that this was my little sister Dora and this was Tomer Janon, a friend of the family. I introduced Arial as a cousin for now, things would get straightened out in the morning.

"We have a couple of cots set up in your room for the young ones; Arial can have your bed. But you get a sleeping bag in the living room for tonight." Henrietta showed Arial where the bathroom was and helped put the youngsters to bed.

Somewhere in between I managed to climb into the sleeping bag, the next thing I remember was the sun shining in my face and the sounds and smells of breakfast.

"Hey there sleepy head, you're still as lazy as ever I

see." That was the old Arial.

"And you're just as bossy as ever. Just remember who the oldest is." I rubbed my eyes and noticed two small children sitting at the dining room table busily eating.

"How are they doing this morning?" I asked her quietly.

Arial sat down on the floor beside me so they couldn't hear us talk.

"Tomer woke up crying, that woke Dora up, and I'm still tired."

"And, if I remember right you're cranky when you're tired as well." I climbed out of the sleeping bag and rolled it up. I was starved. "Let's eat and then we need to start making plans."

CHAPTER 41

Ned was already downstairs working in the store when we finished breakfast. Dora was over talking with Henrietta while Tomer was sitting on the floor playing with a toy he had brought with him. I remembered some of my old things that they had bought for my first Christmas and dug some of the smaller ones out for him. They had been a little young for me back then, but it was all we had.

"If you two have finished scheming, how about telling me who you really are?" Henrietta had finished taking care of the breakfast dishes and was sitting at the table with Dora.

"I suppose we owe you that much, but we should tell it to both of you."

"That won't be a problem Jason" Ned said has he appeared at the top of the stairs. "I put a sign in the store window; this is usually a slow part of the day. Let's hear the real story, from the beginning."

"Dora?" I asked, "Can you keep an eye on Tomer

while we talk in the living room? Just sit where you can see him."

She gave me a dirty look, "I'm not a…"

I gave her a hard look back and she shut up. "Dora, I know exactly how you feel. I went through the same thing five years ago when I was abandoned here."

She sat down on the arm of the couch but still gave me a belligerent look.

"And I want to make sure that you treat our hosts with respect. They took me in and raised me as their own and put up with I don't know how much of my malarkey in that same amount of time." Her eyes softened a little. "You're my little sister and I do love you no matter how awful you act."

"What's malarkey?" she asked.

"One of the many things you're going to have to learn in a hurry if you're going to live around here. Now back to the present matters."

I looked at Ned and Henrietta who sat there patiently waiting. "And from now on we all speak English and thank you Dora for making me learn it."

"As I introduced them last night, this really is my little sister Dora. Our parents' names are Harkinson and Valya Kingston. For all intents and purposes I was an abandoned child when I came here. It was expedient at that time to claim that my parents were dead as they were totally unreachable." which they were.

"The young boy over there is Tomer Janon, his parents' names were Charna and Parmo and I really don't know if they are still alive or not." Henrietta was waiting for the next one. "And this lovely creature here is Arial Haldon, and no, she is not my cousin, but an old friend whose father took extraordinary chances to bring them to me to care for."

"And how did they get to you?" Ned asked.

"And this lovely creature thinks that you should tell them everything." Arial said in Wessar.

I could feel my face flushing as I sternly told her to use English. She just gave me a mischievous smile and before I could say anything, "What he is not telling you is that we are from another star system many light-years from here. Our parents have been captured, Tomer's have been killed, and my father escaped and left us for Jason to take care of while he tries to rescue Jasom's parents."

"Well dear", as Henrietta patted me on the knee, "I suppose we should tell you who we really are as well. Dear me" she sputtered, "my Wessar is a little rusty."

I hadn't noticed that she was speaking in Wessar.

Ned continued, "Arson contacted us back before Jason was brought here. He worked through us to get the deeds and such done. Old man Burke had finished his term of planetary observer and they quote, vanished. I still miss that old buzzard; he made the best moonshine I've ever tasted."

Henrietta slapped him on the arm, "Oh you and your moonshine."

I was astounded. "You knew all about me all this time?" Ned nodded. "Why didn't you tell me?

"Because we were not allowed too, and it would be too easy to slip up. Especially with the local law right across the street." He indicated Hiram Wheeler's place. "Not that he wouldn't have kept our secret. But then it wouldn't have been a secret, would it?" Ned chuckled.

"Well I suppose all of our little secrets are sitting on the table. What do we do next?" I sighed and leaned back into the couch before a horrid thought occurred to me.

"If Dressler is still the truancy officer, and Tomer and Dora aren't in school. How do we handle that?"

"What's a truancy officer and what does it have to do with school?" Arial asked.

I told her the story of my first meeting with Mr. Dressler and Mrs. Martin when I first came here.

"Shouldn't be a problem if they're only visiting" Henrietta said, "We'll just pass them off as newly arrived relatives that are up here to say hello and will be leaving soon. Don't worry about that part, we'll figure something out."

"The real thing is" Ned asked, "What are you going to be doing next?"

"What do you know about the derelict out in the asteroid belt? Everything going on is somehow connected to that."

"Nothing more than rumors so far, some hold the belief that the predecessors landed here and settled this planet." Ned said.

Henrietta picked it up, "There's an ancient legend about an ark that brought them to a promised land. But everything about it is so vague that we've never found any truth in it."

"It's just an empty hulk isn't it?" Ned asked me.

"Arial, why don't you fill them in on what is happening with the derelict, you've been closest to it."

Arial spent the next several minutes explaining all of the work that had been put into removing the asteroid barrier from around the derelict and the subsequent hull mapping. "They haven't managed to open the hatch yet, but they were going to attempt a breach soon."

"What kind of people are in this crew?" I asked her.

"Mostly scientists of low caliber, you know, political flunkies willing to do or say anything to keep their precious jobs. Except for maybe Professor Whinoni. She was only included because they didn't have a qualified linguist. She's a well-known expert on Predecessor artifacts and their language; it is different from Wessar in some very strange ways. Most people just assume that the predecessors spoke Wessar, but from what she tells me it was quite different."

I had the urge to hop into the flyer and try to save

our parents when Ned put his hand on my shoulder. "Don't go flyin' off the handle just yet son. Let's think this thing through first."

"I need some fresh air and a walk. Would you guys mind watching over the youngsters for a little bit?" I got up off the couch and grabbed my jacket by the door. I was halfway down the stairs before I realized I was being followed.

"You're not going to do anything stupid without me are you?" Arial accused me. Because it is not going to happen, I'm tagging along."

Henrietta appeared at the top of the stairs, "Arial dear, you're going to need a jacket as well" As she handed one to her.

We walked down the street to the corner and crossed the tracks. Before long I found myself standing outside the high school.

"What's this place?" Arial asked.

I explained what a school was and all of the classes I had taken as well as what the graduation ceremony meant.

"Why did you let her win?" she asked.

"Let who win?"

"That Holly creature. Why did you let her get the higher marks?"

I smiled remembering how I felt in high school. "Because I didn't want to be noticed, that's all."

"Does she know that you let her win?"

"Oh yes! She knew and she didn't like it either."

"That doesn't make sense. Why didn't she like you?"

"Because it made her feel like she didn't earn it."

"But she didn't. Can't you see that? You gave it to her, she should be grateful."

"Arial. If someone cheated on a test so that you could win, how would you feel?"

"I'd break their head in!" Her face softened a bit. "OH!"

"That's why! She's just like you in that way. I think they call it pride here."

"These earth people are strange."

I just laughed until it hurt and couldn't stop. Her face was so red it almost matched her hair. I thought she was going to hurt me, bad. Than her face cleared as she realized what she had said.

For the rest of the walk we talked about what it had been like coming back and trying to get along with the crew. As time went by they had steadily been pushed out of the way and locked out of any discovery. Dad had foreseen this happening but hadn't been able to stop it. They had been intentionally vague on all of my messages as they knew they were being monitored.

It had finally come to a head when Charna was out examining the propulsion units on the derelict. One of the Tarkna's crew told him to get away from there. Charna couldn't hear him as his comm. unit was defective. Parma had just repaired it and was on her way over to replace it when Charna was shot by the thug. She screamed at him through the comm. and he shot her too.

Arson and dad were furious and said that he was a murderer and should be imprisoned. The crew's captain was apologetic but said there was nothing he could do about it. Dad said that he and Valya were coming over to discuss it and they were taken into custody as they entered the ship. Arson immediately gathered Arial and the children in a flyer and snuck out through the surrounding asteroid field and brought them to me for safety.

"Dad also mentioned something else to me that didn't make much sense at the time." Arial was puzzled, "From what I've learned since I've been here, there are some of our people living here, on this planet. How did they get here, and why are they here?"

"That I can't answer" I replied, "I was startled to find someone talking to me in Wessar at college and then to find out he's your cousin was another shock." I shook my head and shivered. "Now I find out that the people I have been living with for the last five years are our people too…"

By then we were back to the train tracks and just as the crossing guard lights started flashing and the arms dropped across the road. Off to the southeast I could see the morning train approaching.

Just as the horn sounded Arial wrapped her arms around me as the sound of an approaching train sounded from the west. "WHAAAAH!"

"WHAT's that?" she quivered.

"Just the morning train coming through, one in the morning, one in the afternoon, and another about ten o'clock at night. It's almost here; we better back up a little, kicks up a lot of dust as it goes by."

She slowly released her death grip on me as the locomotive approached. It was still amazing to me to listen to the change in sound as it went by. I eventually had learned in science class that it was called the Doppler Effect; the rise in frequency as the train whistle approached and the fall in frequency as it disappeared into the west before vanishing from sight leaving a quiet stillness as if it had never even been there.

We finished walking home without talking very much, I had told her about the farm and how I was using it for income and a place to hide the flyer.

"I wonder where Ned and Henrietta hide their flyer?" Arial mused as we walked along.

I stopped right there. "If they have a flyer, then so should your cousins. I wish I knew where they lived. Maybe we could find out what they are up to."

"Why don't you just ask Ned, he seems to know a lot about who is where."

CHAPTER 42

Later that afternoon I took Arial out to the flyer with me. I spoke with Mrs. Farnham and said I was just out there to pick some things stored in the barn. I introduced Arial as a visiting relative and we talked for a while as her two younger children played outside. After exchanging pleasantries I took Arial into the barn and showed her where the hidden door led into the small area where the flyer was hidden. "There's also a trap door in the floor that I keep locked from this side, it drops into the lower store room."

We crowded into the flyer and while we waited for it to power up, Arial started rummaging in the back.

"What are you doing back there?" I asked her.

"Found it! I was wondering where I had put this" she squealed with delight.

"Found what?" I asked.

"My other suit and helmet, I ran out of room in my locker so I stashed this one in the back locker, and then you ran off with the flyer and I had to buy another one. Now we can go together" as she smiled brightly at me.

"Go where together?" I asked puzzled.

She continued to smile at me, "When do we leave?"

She had trapped me. I was planning on leaving them with Ned and Henrietta and heading out to save mom and dad by myself. With only one suit, only one person could go.

"Beep, Beep", saved by the bell, two messages.

I opened the first one from Dad, Arial was reading over my shoulder.

Jasom, this is to inform you that your mother and I are fine; Arson and Jayla are under house arrest along with the children in the King's Quest. Charna has been injured and is being taken care of in the Tarkna's infirmary, Parmo is with him. We are all doing fine, and the work is proceeding as planned. For now you need to stay where you are, we will be in touch again really soon.

I read it through again, without making any more sense out of it. "What do you think? Is this actually from him or a cleverly disguised forgery? It doesn't sound like dad at all."

"I can't see him saying something like that either. Let's read the other message."

The second one was from Arson.

Jasom, I hope you're doing well with what I've sent you, I know it's not much but it's all I have that I can spare. Jayla and I have been wondering if we will see you soon and hope we can all be reunited again. A little red can be a burden at times.

Arson, Captain, King's Quest

I heard a sniff from behind me and felt a drop of water on my cheek. "I can't believe what I just read" I mused.

"He just said goodbye" Arial said, as she burst into tears.

I rose from the pilots chair and took her in my arms. "There's more in there than that" I told her. "If I read it right, he's expecting us to come to his rescue and I'm sure dad's message is a fake."

"What should we do?" she wailed, slowly calming down.

"I need to answer at least the one from dad. Let them think that I'm sitting here waiting and not letting on that us…no, not us, but I! I can't even hint that the three of you are here. It's just me, all alone here on a planet that has no indication that there is another culture living alongside them and that spaceships are real."

I quickly composed and sent a message back to the effect that I would stay right here waiting for them to come and pick me up when they can. "There, and they don't need to know that I have a flyer either."

"When are we leaving?" she asked, her eyes were still a little red but she'd stopped crying.

"Not yet, should we send one back to your father also?"

Arial thought for a moment, "Yes, he sent a message he deserves to know that you understand what he was hinting at."

I pondered about that for a moment. "OK, how's this?"

Arson, captain King's Quest

Yes sir, received your package and thank you very much for your thoughtfulness. The red is fine and the double fudge goes well with it. If only I had some ice cream to make the sandwich out of. I guess we'll just have to take care of that one personally. Hope to see you soon, I miss our little family.

Jasom Kingston, crew, King's Quest

"Well, what do you think of that? Will it do?"

"I haven't a clue as to what half of that refers to" she replied.

"That's the point. It will confuse whoever is monitoring us without telling them anything. Arson will know that only part of this message really means anything and that we will be coming, and soon."

She thought about it for a moment and then I sent it along. "Stow your suit in with mine; we really should air them out before we take off." I checked my watch, "and we should be heading back as well."

I sat back in the pilot's chair and was about to power the flyer down when another message arrived.

"Beep wissszt!"

I stared at Arial in disbelief. I had never heard that sound before. I opened it up and read the short note.

"Jason, Arial! Beware! We are being watched at home. Use the back way I showed you in through the loading dock. Ned"

"The net is closing around us, some of the people here may be working with the crew from the Tarkna, and they are looking for us."

"Should we try to go back?" Arial asked.

"Yes and no. I have an idea." I left the flyer in stand-by mode, we may have to leave in a hurry, and drove over to the Thatcher house.

CHAPTER 43

Holly was away at school, but I was looking for her brother Billy. He should be in his room doing homework. Mrs. Thatcher was surprised when she let us in.

"Why what are you doing home Jason" she remarked. "Aren't you supposed to be at college? Holly didn't mention any day off."

"No, things are fine, I just had some distant relatives come for a quick visit, I'll be headed back probably by tomorrow. Is Billy home?"

"Oh, yes I'll get him."

We said hello and I introduced Arial and we walked out of the house to talk while Mrs. Thatcher talked with Arial.

"Billy, can you do me a big favor right now?"

He looked back at the house with a faint smile on his face, "does it involve Arial?"

"Yes it does" I lied.

"Count me in. What do I have to do?"

It took him a minute to convince his mother that he wouldn't be long, but I know she was suspicious.

"OK, now what do I have to do?"

"Did you bring the bat?" He nodded. "Give it to Arial." He did and she just looked at it with a questioning look on her face.

I gave her a quick smile and continued with Billy.

"What I need you to do is very dangerous, there are people around here looking for us and I need to check on Ned and Henrietta."

"OK" he replied lamely.

"Remember when we would play basketball by my garage?"

"Yeah, that was a lot of fun."

"Well, right around behind the garage is where the trucks back up to the loading dock. Right in the corner of the building is a plain door. It's locked, but the key is on top of the door casing. Unlock the door and go upstairs and ask if everything is alright. It's just the two of them and two young children. Make sure things are OK and come right back here and wait for me. Got it?"

"You bet" he replied and smiled at Arial.

Before I could stop her she reached across and kissed him on the cheek, "and that's for luck."

He blushed a little and scurried through the brush and across the tracks to the back of the store.

"In case someone is watching, we're going to move

further up the road and watch what happens." Quietly we slipped through the brush to where we could get a better view of the loading dock.

Billy's dark clothing made him hard to see until he got to the door. I could make out his outline reaching up for the key and slipping inside the door. The door closed behind him and then all we had to do was wait. That was never one of my better traits, and Arial was even worse.

Five minutes later I saw the door open again and a dark figure slowly walked across the tracks. As I feared it wasn't Billy. The figure approached where I had parked Ned's car. It was dark so he couldn't see if anyone was inside.

"You know what to do?" She nodded and we parted in opposite directions.

The figure glanced up from the car to see a dark hooded figure approaching him.

"You're a hard one to find mister." the stranger called.

"And just whom do you think you are talking too" I replied in as hoarse a voice as I could muster.

"Heh, I know who you are, you're Jason Kingston. I've been sent to bring you to Hawthorne."

"So you are one of those heathen low lifers that tore up my nice farm? Why would I want to go anywhere with you? Why don't you just start crawling back to Hawthorne and tell him if he wants to talk to me he'll have to come to me. Go!" I commanded, pointing back across the tracks." Back where you came from."

"We've got the Johnson's and their kids" he snarled.

"Do you now?" I laughed at him. He never saw Arial slip up behind him with a baseball bat. He probably never felt the ground come up to greet him either.

We tied him up and stuffed him in the trunk.

"What's next" Arial asked.

I didn't say it, because I hadn't a clue. I did know that we had to get them out of there. "How hard did you hit him?"

"Not very, this thing is clumsy; I didn't want to split his skull open."

I heard a groan from the trunk, "Follow my lead, I think we just might be able to scare him enough to get what we need out of him."

I poked him a little and he squirmed. "Hey! Wake up sleepy head." as Arial poked him with the bat. "Next time I'll not hold her back, she gets real irritable when I don't let her have her way." I heard a snarl beside me and wasn't sure who it was intended for. "She wanted to bust your brains out and I might just let her if you don't tell me what I need to know." I got down real close and gave him a toothy smile. "Which will it be?"

Arial got down in his face next. I couldn't see what she did, but I did see him cringe. "It won't go well with Hawthorne."

"Hawthorne is next" I replied in a drool voice. "You earthlings are such easy prey."

"I think he might make a tasty stew." Arial added.

"Stew? You aren't from Earth? Where are you from, Mars? Why are you here?"

"SILENCE!" I commanded. "So, he's told you where we're from, too bad. How many more morsels are with him? We might just spare you if you are useful."

I watched the color drain from his face.

"Oh, I can be very useful, yes, yes, very useful." He licked his lips. "There's just Hawthorne and Rickers with him in the house. The old man left a couple of hours ago.

"What old man?" I commanded.

"The one we call chief, lived across the road. He's the one that got us in the house. He said he was going to get the others. Is that being useful?" he quivered.

"Very much so, sleep well my morsel" and I pinched off the nerve on the side of his head and put him to sleep.

"Who's the old man?" Arial asked.

"Supposedly an old friend I thought, but then again Ned didn't trust him, don't suppose I should either."

"What now" she asked.

I simply answered, "We're going in."

CHAPTER 44

The clouds were rolling in and a cold wind was starting to blow as I led us further along the tracks to cross behind the bakery shop. That would put us out of sight of the store. We needed to get inside without being heard or seen and there was only one way to do it. We couldn't use the same door Billy used, once inside we would be sitting ducks; we needed another way in.

Once, a long time ago I had found a small doorway under the dock that led into a crawl space. From inside there was another access door into the lower storage area where the non-perishables were stored. I don't think that Ned even knew about this and I had only discovered it by accident while exploring one day.

I opened the access door and shone my flashlight inside, there were cobwebs everywhere.

"What being lives in there?" Arial asked.

"This time of year, none that I know of." I grabbed a stick and collected most of them as we made our way inside. Arial pulled the door closed behind us and we used our flashlights to crawl over to the other door.

I fumbled with the latch, and opened the door just enough to see that it was dark inside. We slipped inside and closed the door. I took her hand and wound my way between the stacks of crates and boxes and up the landing that led up to the main floor of the store.

Ned may not have known of that way in, but he had shown me one other odd thing about this building. It had a second stairway to the second floor that had been closed off when they moved in. The lower doorway was behind the Walk-in cooler. It was a tight fit to get back there, and we had to be quiet on the stairs as they hadn't been used in many years. The door at the top was part of my bedroom wall.

At the top I listened carefully for any trace of sound but didn't hear any. I couldn't remember if there was anything up against it or not. I was just about to try pushing it when Arial whispered in my ear.

"Did you know there's a little crack in this door and I can see inside the room. This is your bedroom isn't it?"

"Was last time I lived here" I whispered back, "can you see anything?"

"Yes, Tomer is lying quietly on his cot, he appears to be asleep." she continued looking around the room limited by the size of the opening. "Oh, there she is. Dora has something in her hand and is waiting to use it on the first person coming through this door. She has heard us coming up the stairs. She's very smart you know."

"I know she's smart, she takes after me. Watch this." I started tapping lightly on the door panel using a code we used to have when we were playing on the King's Quest.

I waited a moment and repeated it. "What's she doing now?"

"She seems puzzled but she put that thing down."

Then I heard a light tapping on the wall off to the right. "Yes! She remembered." And I started tapping what she needed to do.

I gently opened the door and motioned her to be very quiet. "First" I whispered in her ear, "We're going to get you and Tomer out of here."

She gave me a rebellious look until I told her she had to protect Tomer and I wasn't going to abandon them either. She gently woke Tomer and we took them back down the stairway and into the lower storage area. I showed her how to get out but couldn't think of anyone to send them to until I remembered about Billy.

"Dora, how many people are there upstairs besides Ned and Henrietta?"

"Only three, one of them calls himself something like Hawthorne, the others are just thugs."

"Good, have you seen another young man show up recently?"

"There was a disturbance about a half hour or so

ago, but I couldn't see what was going on. They locked us in the bedroom and Tomer cried himself to sleep" she replied sadly.

"I'm glad he's got someone like you to watch over him" I told her.

"Now what do we do?" Arial asked.

"Something I saw done in a movie once, it's just crazy enough to work. Wait here, I'll be right back."

I quickly stole back up the stairs and wedged the bedroom door so it couldn't be opened easily. Then I dug around in the bottom of the closet for one of the old presents that Ned had bought me that first year and then back down the stairs.

"Dora, you stay here with Tomer. Arial, bring the bat." And I headed out onto the loading dock to the door that led upstairs.

"Aye, aye, sir" she whispered as she followed me across the loading dock.

The side staircase was the only other way to get upstairs. It was also the only way to get back down. If we can't get up we'll get them when they come down. I peeked around the corner and looked up the stairs. The kitchen door was ajar and I could hear voices. I could also hear Billy crying and Henrietta trying to soothe him. I could also hear Hawthorne harassing Ned.

There was only one light in the stairway. I pulled out the bag of marbles and the slingshot and took aim. I was just about to let fly when Hawthorne bellowed to Rickers to go see what was keeping Rawson. That must be the guy in the trunk, never thought to ask his name. I pulled back and closed the door locking it from our side. I kept my ear close to the door and listened for Rickers to come down the stairs.

"What's happening?" Arial asked.

"Rickers is going to be coming down the stairs, I don't think we can take him unless it's by surprise."

"How do I get outside?"

"Well, usually through this door, turn right, down a few stairs and out the door."

Before I could say any more she was through the door, down the stairs and out onto the walkway, slamming the door behind her. I belatedly tried to stop her and in my confusion I spilled the bag of marbles onto the rug on the landing, I grabbed a handful and quickly closed the door as I heard Rickers coming down the stairs in a hurry.

"Hey you!" he shouted just as he hit the landing.

The next thing I heard was a big crash and the outside door rattling. I stole a quick look through the door, Rickers was crumpled up in a ball at the foot of the stairs. Then the door opened and Arial reached in and dragged him out into the darkness. Above I could hear Hawthorne yelling after him. I took quick aim and missed the light. It bounced off the casing and slowly descended the stairs ending up back on the carpet. I took aim again and let fly just as Hawthorne stuck his head out the door. I missed the light again, and nailed him right in the forehead. He stumbled a little and fired his gun. I had pulled back just in time as the shot hit the casing over my head. I locked the door and headed for the doorway off the dock. I heard him coming down the stairs and I wasn't about to be there when he got to the door. I didn't bother to close the outside door behind me as I headed toward the garage.

Just as I came around the corner I stumbled over an inert body. I glanced down expecting to see Arial lying there dead. Instead it was Rickers bound, gagged, and still unconscious. Ten stairs down head first in free fall, it's a wonder he didn't break his neck.

Just then there was another loud crash followed by a loud thunk. Arial hollered at me. "Get over here and help me tie this one up, He was about to point some weapon at me and I didn't hold back this time."

There was a slight trickle of blood running down the side of his head where she had beaned him with the bat. We trussed him up really tight and went through his clothing looking for any other weapons including knives of any sort. We came up with four revolvers and six knives. I made sure their wrists were tightly bound behind them as well as their ankles.

"Now what commander" Arial's amused comment reminded me that I had started with no plan and still didn't have one.

"Now it's upstairs to make sure everybody's OK, then we have a pow-wow."

She gave me the strangest look. "I don't think I know you anymore."

I gave her a foolish grin and we headed back upstairs.

In the kitchen everyone was sitting around the table with their hands tied behind their backs. Henrietta was shocked when she saw us come in through the door.

"Don't worry, they're all tied up at the moment and will probably wake up with splitting headaches later on." Arial was standing beside me nonchalantly holding the bat in her hands. "Oh and you better watch your step on the lower landing, I spilled a bag of marbles on the rug."

"Would have loved to see that happen" Ned chuckled. "We were worried when the gun fire started. It's a wonder the neighbors aren't over here already."

We untied them and Henrietta headed to the bedrooms, "Where are the children?" She hollered back.

"They're fine; we left them in the lower storage room. Would the neighbors call the police?"

"Don't have any" he replied, "But they might have called the local sheriff, he lives over in Wolf Point, probably take him about an hour to get here."

"Jason, Hiram's one of them ain't he?"

"Yes Ned, I'm afraid he is the boss and knows all about you and Henrietta. Arial? Do you remember what your uncle looks like? That would be Jared's father."

"I haven't seen him in over ten years, not enough to describe him" she relied.

"Ned, do you have the keys to his house yet? Let's have a look at what he's got stored over there."

"What about the children?" Henrietta wanted to know. "It isn't safe for them here anymore."

I had forgotten Billy was standing there trying to keep up with what we were talking about. "Uh, maybe I could talk mom into taking them in for the night?" he volunteered.

"Let me call her, she must be getting worried about you being out so late. Jason get the children up here, now." as she went off to call Mrs. Thatcher.

Dora was peeved at me for leaving them there in the dark so long but I didn't give her a chance to complain. "Come on, we've got to move you two somewhere safer" as I hustled them back up the stairs. At the landing I shooed them up the stairs while I got all the marbles back into the bag which I stuck in my coat pocket; the slingshot was on the other side.

Billy was still standing there eyeing Arial. Poor kid he was in for a shock, and so was I.

"It's all set" Henrietta said as she hung up the phone, "I told her that Billy had been a big help and that we had trouble with the store and we'd be closed for a few days. I talked her into taking us in for the night. Billy will you help me get the children over to your house?"

At the bottom of the stairs Arial gave Billy a big hug and told him how he was such a big hero. In the darkness I couldn't see his face turn red as they walked up the street to the Thatcher's house.

"You're just going to break his heart, you know?"

"Whatever greases the wheel" she replied.

"And what goes around comes around. Watch yourself."

"OK Ned, what do we do next?" I had no idea what to do, I just knew I had to do something and now.

"Where's your flyer, in the barn?" he asked.

"Yes, but it's a tight squeeze for two." Then I thought, "Where's your flyer Ned?"

"We came in a larger convoy; all we have is a pick-up point. But I do have a transmitter in the cellar. I'll start putting a message together now, where's the car?"

"Other side of the tracks and Rawson is sleeping in the trunk. I'll go bring it around and we'll lock the three of them up until the sheriff gets here."

I ran back to the car and quickly drove it back to the store. Ned and Arial had dragged the still unconscious thugs into the garage and gagged them as well. I opened up the trunk and Rawson stared back at me. "Well, well, well, my little morsel is awake." I just couldn't resist watching his face turn pale. "You have been quite helpful and you shall be properly rewarded."

At that point Arial gave him a very strange smile and licked here lips. "He looks really tasty; can I make him into a stew yet?"

"Not yet, my pet, he is still useful, aren't you my little Morsel?" I kissed her cheek. "Are the others prepared?"

"As you commanded my dear" she replied giving Rawson another appraising look. "But I still like him the best."

"Later my dear, we still need to know where the old man went." I watched Rawson carefully.

"If I tell you would you let me go?"

"Go? Go where?" I knelt down and looked him right in the eye. "Where ever he has gone, he will be coming back. Won't he?" I growled at him.

He squirmed a little. "Yes, he has gone down to Billings, he should be back day after tomorrow."

"I don't believe you!" I snarled at him. "My dear, perhaps it is time for a stew after all." Arial squealed in delight and I thought Rawson was going to pass out from fright.

"All right, all right" he cried. "Old man Haldon will be back tomorrow with the rest of his family. There's some big thing happening and they need to leave soon but they wanted to make sure no one would be left to know that they were ever here."

"So uncle Garlo is here." Arial pondered on that thoughtfully. I let her play it out.

"He's your uncle?" Rawson's eyes were very big.

"And he just loves you earthlings, such nice stew."

This time his eyes rolled up out of sight and he went completely limp. We rolled him out of the trunk and dragged him into the garage with the others. Rickers was awake and watching us.

"You should be more careful who you associate with, this guy thinks we're Martians. What a fruitcake." Ricker just looked at Rawson then back up to me. I gave him a sly smile. There'll be someone alone shortly to pick you up. Relax, you'll be safer in jail, next time either of us see you, you'll get what he did." A little tinkling laugh from Arial and we left them in the darkness of the garage.

"Message all sent" Ned said as he joined us outside the garage, "it may take them a while, but they'll be here soon".

"Ned, can you give us a lift out to the farm? We have to go now before it's too late and you need to be here when the sheriff gets here. Take care of Henrietta and the kids, we'll be back as soon as we can."

As we drove into the yard at the farm, a light came on at the porch. Shortly a young man approached us and Ned went to talk to him. I unlocked the big barn doors and opened up the boarded up wall; Arial was inside the flyer.

Ted Farnham shook my hand and then spoke in Wessar. "Jason, I don't know all that's going on, but we wish you a safe journey." His wife waved from the porch as Arial slowly drove the flyer out into the drive way.

I climbed in beside Arial and put my suit on. Slowly she took us up through the atmosphere as we headed out toward Mars. From there we would sneak up on the King's Quest.

CHAPTER 45

"Are you sure about the coordinates?" I asked her.

"Yes, I memorized them before we left, we should be out of detector view if we stay on the outer edge of the main ring. I'm getting a few blips now, we must be getting close."

This was not the way you're supposed to approach your base station, but we didn't want to be detected and we were running with as little propulsion as possible. It was hectic, squeezing between this boulder and then the next one.

"I've got some stronger signals coming in, we're almost there."

"Hey! Up ahead, isn't that our old friend Alpha-1?" I pointed off toward the left.

"Yup! Hold her steady and see if you can anchor us to the side. I'll run up to the edge and take a quick look." Arial headed out the back and closed the inner door on the airlock. I quickly evacuated the chamber as she tied off the safety line outside the hatch and closed the door. I left it empty, but with the hatch closed I could follow her if needed.

I watched her scramble carefully up to the edge using claws built into her gauntlets and dragging the line behind her. I resisted the urge to join her, but we had agreed that one of us should always be at the controls. There was a blip on the detector and I was checking it out when I heard the outer hatch close. I opened the valve and pressurized the airlock.

"Here's the video, run it through while I make a quick call to the fresher."

I ran her video feed through the compressor algorithm and we gazed at the scene. The king's Quest and Tarkna were tied off to adjacent asteroids. The algorithm generated all of the measurements from her video feed so we could determine just how far each object was from its neighbor.

"Did you leave a repeater in their line of sight?" I asked her.

"Should be on channel 43, no one ever seems to use that one, and it's a very low power directional feed. If it does bounce around and they hear it hopefully they won't be able to follow it back to here."

"Step two, listen in on them, discover routines, and try to find who's where."

"Sniff! Starting to smell in here." she remarked.

"And it's going to get worse until we can get our air recycled. And there's only one place near here." I gazed longingly at the open flyer hanger bay. It was on the side away from the Tarkna.

"You're not thinking what I think you're thinking are you?"

"What about if I can sneak inside, and then you dock the flyer. When someone comes to see who it is, I'll jump on them." It sounded so simple. After all, the thing with the marbles worked out didn't it?

"You're nuts!"

"You like the way we smell?"

"We better do this fast then before I change my mind."

But I didn't get that far.

"Beep!" The receiver went.

"Do they know we're here or is this just another message and they think we're still in Montana?"

Arial thought for a moment, "Why don't we just read it and find out?"

The message was from Arson explaining that he, Jayla, and the children were being left alone but Harkinson and Valya where helping out on the Tarkna. He hoped that I was doing OK and they were sending someone to bring me back home.

"He's a little late on that one, but if we can believe that they're not under guard then we should move now."

"Do you think that we could get the flyer serviced and get back out here without being seen? There is so much we could be doing as long as they don't know we're here. Once they find out that you're here they'll close in on us.

There is no such thing as a foolproof plan, and there was the old saying I had heard about the best laid plans of mice and men. "Let me go first. I'll say nightmare if I run into problems and…"

"Let's not get to complicated, just broadcast my name. They already think I'm still there."

CHAPTER 46

I couldn't use a lifeline for this trip, just small bursts of propulsion. I picked my route staying in the shadows so there wouldn't be any reflections and always out of sight of both ships. It took nearly an hour and I was almost halfway through my tank of air before I crawled into the open flyer bay.

I knew where all of the sensors were and stole inside without being noticed. The airlock was manual and I cycled myself through, hanging my suit to the rack on the wall; the next time I needed it, it would be completely refreshed.

I couldn't wear my old ship suit so I was hoping I could find one of dad's. It was very quiet in the hallways as I headed up into our bedroom area. I found one of his ship suits and put it on rolling up my earth clothes and stuffing them in a corner.

Over by his desk I turned on the internal comm. and listened to see what was going on. I could hear Arson talking with someone about the work sight but nothing else. There was a noise in the hallway outside and I hid on the floor just as the door opened.

I was in the dark, but I could see by the mirror over the bureau that Jayla was standing in the doorway staring into the darkness. I was about to let her know I was there when a strange voice behind her asked her what she was doing.

"I was just going to pick up something of Valya's for her." Jayla replied in a meek voice.

"Well she ain't going to need it much longer. Back to your station."

Jayla nodded at the mirror, she had seen me, before slowly closing the door. I didn't hear the latch click and there was a sliver of light showing through. She was setting him up for me. I searched through the desk until I remembered that I still had my slingshot and bag of marbles.

I only had one chance. I slowly opened the door enough to see who was where and pulled the band back as far as I dared. I braced against the door frame, this was going to hurt when it hit.

"Thwack!" Whoever it was slowly turned around to face me. "I'm dead" I thought, and then he slowly slithered to the floor.

Quietly Jayla helped me drag him into the bedroom and we quickly tied his hands and feet and stuffed a gag in his mouth.

"He's going to make a lot of racket when he wakes up" Jayla said, "Just what is that thing anyway."

I stood up and she stared at me. "My how you've changed! Arson said you'd be a lot more grown next time we would see you."

"How many more are there?" I asked her quickly.

"He's the only one here with us, but his replacement will be coming in about another hour. Where's Arial and the children?" she asked anxiously.

"The children are with friends and Arial's waiting in the flyer; I'll have her dock the flyer. You go tell Arson so he can cover for us if we need it."

She disappeared down the passageway and I went back to the airlock. I used a low power signal pointed in the general direction and just spoke her name. She must have been close as I had to sprint for the door as she brought the flyer in faster than I would have ever dared.

She was good at it though, hardly made a noise until the clamps engaged. Then she was out of it and headed to the airlock. I let her go through, I knew where she was headed, then quickly hooked up the recharge cycle on the flyer and headed down the corridor to find Arson.

CHAPTER 47

The four of us gathered in the rec room after taking care of the thug I had brained with the slingshot. "If we're going to do anything" I pressed, "we should be doing it now. Time is not on our side and there are other players, and they're beginning to close in on us."

"What Jason is saying is true." Arial piped in quickly. "Uncle Garlo has been living on this planet for many years along with many other parties we didn't even know about. We need to close in before they get here."

"Hold on Arial" her mother commanded, "you have no concept of what is happening out there. Listen to your father."

"Well Arson?" I asked dryly, "Should we just sit here and wait for them to show up and watch which side they land on?" I pressed him as it was going to be his decision regardless of what I wanted to do.

Arson looked like the weight of the world was on his shoulders, was he up to the job I wondered?

"There's a lot of merit to what you're saying Jason, but we just can't go rushing in there."

I knew he was just being cautious, and I admired that about him. He had setup my entire background before putting me on planet Earth and it had worked admirably. "Tell me about the situation on the Tarkna. How many people are there and what are they like?"

He leaned back in the chair. "I've only been over there a couple of times after we first arrived. They were a little hostile then and it only got worse. Let's start with the captain." He listed each of the personnel aboard and their background.

"Captain Hadley is loyal to his ship and his crew, basically. He could be pushed either way depending on the situation. Two of his four crew members, Chief Polland, and the mate, Rastern, are loyal to the captain; whichever way he goes they will follow. The other two crew members have been replaced with council thugs; we have one of them tied up for the moment and the other will be showing up here before too long." Hopefully the same tactic would work on him.

"Of the scientists, Dr. LeOnard was a well-respected authority on predecessor artifacts. He staunchly was against there being any merit in this expedition. I haven't had the chance to see if he's changed his mind yet."

"Along with him is Professor Whinoni. She is one of the best known linguists anywhere. She and Dr. LeOnard are the only ones that lend any credence to this mission."

"Dr. Obehail is a professional toe licker and is willing to add his credibility to anything that some members of the council want to put off as fact. He and his assistant Monuha are here to sabotage the mission if it suits their councilors favor. It would be best just to shove them out the air lock first chance we get."

"Arson!" Jayla looked shocked.

"What's the matter Jayla? I've heard you say worse about them many times."

"We need to get inside and find out what is going on with mom and dad as well." I was anxious to get going. "Have they managed to open the ship yet?"

"Not that I'm aware of. Obehail would probably have had us tossed aside already, but he suspects we haven't told him everything that we know. That's the only reason we're still alive. He's already had Charna and Parmo killed. He's holding Harkinson and Valya as a wedge against us." He jumped up and walked out the door and up the hallway.

"Oh dear, now he's upset again" Jayla said concerned for her husband.

"Stay here" I told them, "I'll speak with him."

I caught up with him at the pilots' station gazing across at the Tarkna. In between there was a small speck slowly moving closer.

"That will be the other thug, Cromer, coming to

relieve his brother Salner." He seemed deep in thought. "They're councilor GraMorn's nephews. They aren't too sharp, but they are tough."

His thoughts turned back toward me. "There's much we need to talk about, especially dealing with Arial, and the children" he added quickly. "Just how did you knock Salner out anyway?"

I showed him the bag of marbles and the sling-shot.

"That looks dangerous to people, but perfect for aboard ship. Think you can do it again?" he asked.

"Not without a backup, I hope Arial brought the bat with her."

We were both in place just out of sight from where he would have to hang up his suit. That would be the only time he would be most vulnerable. Arson would be sitting in the pilots chair; I would be just to the side and Arial behind him. As a further backup, Jayla had Salner's gun. I wasn't sure how good she could handle it but she wouldn't be left out.

CHAPTER 48

What can I say, it almost didn't work. Good thing we had a backup for the backup plan. I was ready when Cromer appeared at the door and took my shot and missed. Well not completely, it missed him by a good margin and happened to bounce off the door frame and hit his head enough to make him stagger back. Just as he reached for his gun Arial tried to bean him on the back of the head. Unfortunately, she didn't compensate for the lower ceiling and hit his gun arm instead. As he swung around to shoot her, Jayla nailed him between the eyes with the other gun. He dropped in his tracks as we all looked at each other in disbelief and what we had just done.

"Nice shot Jayla" Arson complimented her as he slowly took the gun from her.

She started saying some really unmentionable things about Cromer and the rest of his family.

"There is no way to stop now. If we're careful this should be the last death."

Arial whispered in my ear. "He was the one that killed Tomer's parents. Mom was really upset about that and the responsibility falls squarely on Dr. Obehail, and he is going to pay dearly."

I'd never heard her sound so dangerously angry, she sounded just like her mother.

"Whatever we do next, it has to be soon" Arson said, "Salner is supposed to be headed back as soon as Cromer gets here. I think his suit will fit me."

Jayla wasn't about to be left behind, "Arson! You're not going to leave me here alone are you? Not with that thug tied up back there, what if he gets loose?"

Arial tried to calm her down. "Mom, someone has to stay here and make like nothing's happened." She then grabbed my arm and we headed toward the flyer bay.

We donned our suits and proceeded with our plan to sneak up on them from the other side. They were down both thugs, and I hoped that that would tip the scales in our favor if we could only keep the element of surprise.

Arial backed the flyer out of its cradle and we slipped around behind the ship and out of sight. We were half way around when I spotted Arson drifting back to the Tarkna in Salner's suit.

"Is this the best place to leave the flyer? I don't like the idea of leaving it unguarded." We had argued on the way over and it boiled down to both of us crawling our way over the rock. "OK, this is the best I can do" As I tied a short line around a rock to keep it from drifting away. Nothing around here had enough gravity to hold a grain of sand much less a space flyer.

Slowly we crawled over the top of the asteroid and were rewarded with a view of the top of the Tarkna projecting above the next asteroid over. Good, that would make it harder to find where we left it. "Take a good fix on the flyer, we may be in a hurry coming back." I carefully watched the objects around me to get an idea of how they were moving until I was sure I could find it again. If not, we could always ping it, but then everyone else would know where it was too. The object was to keep it's presence a secret.

Arson had some basic plans of the layout of the Tarkna, it was very similar to the King's Quest, only somewhat bigger with more cargo space. Our only chance to get inside without being seen was to slip in through an empty cradle. Slowly we crawled over the intervening asteroid to the other side. It was nearly an hour before we slipped over the side and gazed at the shadowed side of the ship.

I keyed my radio to listen for anything going on. Arial held up a hand and showed seven fingers so I switched over to channel 7. I was surprised to see that it wasn't about Arson. "Dr. Obehail, we're sending Salner over to help you out."

What to do? Has the captain taken our side? Was it a setup to pull us in?

"This is Captain Hadley calling the King's Quest,

come in?"

"Captain, this is the King's Quest responding, what is your request?" Jayla replied.

"I need to speak with your captain, immediately, one of our crew members has disappeared and we need some assistance at the derelict. Would you inform him and please ask for his presence at the sight."

"I will inform him of your request Captain Hadley, how soon do you require his presence?"

"It should be soon King's Quest, and we are expecting reserves within the next three days."

"May I tell him whom to expect?"

"I'm not sure, the council has approved a small cargo ship of supplies, but I wouldn't be surprised to find more personnel arriving as well. Tarkna out."

"Very well Tarkna, King's Quest out."

I ran an intercom clip between Arial's suit and mine; these were useful for private conversations outside of the ship and couldn't be monitored.

"I'm confused. I thought they'd have imprisoned my father as soon as he stepped out of his suit. I'm not so sure if we should focus on entering the ship or trying to capture Obehail?" Arial remarked.

"Obehail is useless without access to the ship; the ship is our first concern. And who was the figure that left the ship and headed out to the derelict?" I was watching the side of the ship and noticed that there was a slightly darker outline where one of their flyers would be docked.

"I say let's try to get inside and assess the situation. It's either that or head back to the flyer. You see that darker opening about halfway up the side, about where a flyer would dock? Let's see if we can get in through there."

Arial nodded assent as she unclipped the intercom line. We still had our safety line connected, I pulled her close beside me and energized my propulsion unit just enough to head us toward the Tarkna and the open flyer cradle.

I guided us across the open space to the edge of the opening and locked a line on a clip beside the cradle. Arial pulled up tight and let my line pay out enough where I could look inside. The cradle bay was empty with only a low level light on by the airlock door.

I reached around inside the opening and caught a hand hold and pulled us inside and over to the airlock. This was a bigger ship and the airlock could hold three or four people, but should we go in together or separately?

Not my decision, Arial shoved me inside and pulled the outside door closed behind us. There was no way we'd make it inside without an alarm going off so we stowed our suits. I still had my sling-shot and marbles and somehow she had managed to bring along her bat.

I slowly opened the door and looked into the corridor outside. It was empty. I stepped into the corridor and moved quietly down toward the center level. Arial had crept out as soon as I told her it was empty and went the other way toward the infirmary.

CHAPTER 49

Ahead was the Control Room and I could hear voices talking inside. One of them was Captain Hadley, I didn't recognize the other but it was probably Chief Polland.

"Sounds like he's back." Polland's voice called out louder, "Rastern! What took so long. You were supposed to come right back after taking…"

Polland looked up as I stepped inside with my sling-shot armed and loaded.

"Uh, Captain? We have company."

The captain turned from his control board to gaze at me. "And just who the…"

"He's my son captain, and I'd suggest you do as you're told." A cold hard voice came from behind me. I recognized my father's voice but I've never heard him speak with such steely brittleness before.

"Good work son" as he patted me on the back and moved around to stand in front of me facing the captain.

"It is time, Captain Hadley, to make up your mind.

Bow to your renegade councilor's pet, or do the right thing and help us put the murderers in jail. What's it going to be?"

"I'm not sure I understand what's going on here Dad? Wasn't Cromer responsible for the killings?"

"How much do you know young man?" Captain Hadley asked.

"From what I've gathered, it was Cromer that killed Tomer's parents and he and Salner work for Dr. Obehail. Is that correct?" I asked.

"There's more going on here than that son" dad added, "Dr. Obehail's mission is to destroy the derelict."

"What!" I exploded. "Why destroy the one thing that could help determine who the Predecessors were?" I looked back at the captain. "And you're in on this?"

An evil thought occurred to me. "What hold does he have on you?"

"Don't be too harsh on him son, he just hasn't realized the full impact of the situation and its inevitable end, yet!"

"Well captain" I looked him right in the eye, "There's a few less players in this game, Cromer's dead and Salner's tied up at the moment. Whether you know it or not, it wasn't Salner you sent over to Dr. Obehail, it was Captain Arson; seems that he's more of a captain than you are."

Captain Hadley turned red and Polland reached for a weapon, but I was quicker, and this time I didn't miss.

The captain looked shocked as Polland's head snapped back from the marble's impact; his limp body sliding out of the chair to lay in a heap on the floor.

"This place feels deserted, and where is mom? They can't all be out at the work site."

"The good doctor was made chief scientist by the council, but Monuha is only masquerading as his assistant. He takes Valya along to keep me in line. What happened with Cromer?" Dad wanted to know.

"Long story, short form is that Jayla took great pleasure in putting one right between his eyes. We tied Salner up inside one of the airlocks. If he struggles too much the door opens and he's free to leave."

Dad was aghast at my reply. "My word son, what have those heathens taught you?"

I smiled back at him. "I had a very interesting five years living with a very nice older couple. Another long story, for later on."

Suddenly, several pieces of the puzzle fell into place. I spoke to dad but kept my eye on Captain Hadley. I'd already pulled another marble out of the bag and flexed it a few times where the captain could see me.

"It's also given me plenty of time to think about this joyous little planet you marooned me on. It wasn't an accident, was it? You and Arson planned on leaving me there so there would be a reason for you to come back."

"Not exactly, son. It wasn't my idea but Arson and

your mothers. I didn't like the idea but went along with it reluctantly and I don't think that Jayla knows either."

"So" I began, "we're the only four on board and everyone else is at the derelict site. Why don't we just place Polland here where he can have the same decision as Salner?"

I saw a muscle twitch in Polland's face. "Chief Polland" I called, "If you would like another headache I can assist you. But I would much prefer you came along quietly. Behave and you will live to return home."

His eyes opened and he slowly crawled to his feet with a rebellious look on his face. The captain spoke to him and he relaxed.

"Maybe we should make our position clear" I began, "If Dr. Obehail is successful in destroying the derelict, your purpose in this venture, along with the rest of us, will just be a loose end."

Polland seemed confused by what I had said but dad elaborated. "What he means is: if the derelict is destroyed, the only person going back will be Monuha. He might take the doctor along or he might not. But the rest of us will be left here without a ship."

"Is that understandable?" I asked Captain Hadley.

"I was told to do this mission without an understanding about what was involved. You asked earlier what hold he had on me…"

"No need captain" I replied grimly, "We're going to

do what is necessary to put an end to this." I nodded to Polland. "Chief Polland, if you don't mind?"

"May I say my piece first?" he replied.

"Sure, why not" I replied, "which of the other two groups, that are about to enter the picture do you belong too?"

"Sorry captain, but this mission was doomed from the beginning. Harkinson, you've got quite a boy there." Polland looked me over closely. "Garlo said you were a smart one."

"And you still haven't told me whose side you're on." I replied warily. "How soon before we can expect them to arrive?"

"I'd be guessing, but I don't think that they'll get here very soon. They have no idea where the derelict is and neither the captain nor Arson have been broadcasting its location." Polland pondered, "Which brings me back to you!"

"You're wondering how I know where the derelict is?" and I smiled at him. "I'm the one that found it. You think I'd ever forget something like that?"

Dad had been listening closely. "Son, you said there were two other parties. I take it that one of them is Garlo Haldon? He and his family were banished from Renland many years ago. You're saying that they've been living here on Earth all these years?"

"Yes dad, but not unobserved. It seems that there's

a contingent of observers that have been living here for many years. I'd been living with them and didn't even know it until recently. I'm sure that they already knew about the Garlo's little plan of conquest."

"Captain Hadley?" Dad turned his attention back to the captain, "Have you made up your mind? Otherwise we'll put both you and Polland in the airlock. Don't need anybody sneaking up behind us."

In the end we put both of them in the airlock bound and gagged with a trip line to the exhaust valve. I demonstrated how effective the simple connection was, struggle to much and the valve will open. "Of course, as before, once the valve has exhausted all of the air in the airlock, you are both free to leave." I made an expressive gesture; Polland gulped.

CHAPTER 50

Moments later dad and I cycled through the auxiliary airlock.

"It's quicker with a flyer" dad said, "but it's not too far to just float over and also they won't see us coming as easily."

"OK, but I have to do something first." I turned around and focused on the King's Quest. "Jayla?"

"Jayla here. Proceed, confirmed."

Dad gave me a funny look. He moved over beside me and I clipped the intercom wire to his helmet.

"I'll explain it later." as we slowly floated over toward the derelict site. Once upon the crest of the last asteroid, we could look into the cleared space where a large space tug was moored against the side of the derelict along with the missing flyer from the Tarkna. It would act as a home away from home housing space for ten people and supplies enough to hold them through any emergency.

"Alpha Hotel? Over."

"Jasom, Arson, confirmed, over." Came the quick reply. Shortly there were several other shorter responses. "JK, confirmed, over."

"Who are you talking too?" Dad asked.

"It's more than whom; the responses are preprogrammed into several repeaters that have been scattered around the area. It also tells me that they know about Arson, his response was different."

Dad chuckled in response. "Let's go get your mother out of there."

I unclipped the intercom connection and was just about to move forward when I felt a tap on my shoulder. I turned around and was staring into the wrong end of a nasty looking weapon.

Dad turned around and the figure moved back to cover both of us. I couldn't see who was inside, but the weapon looked real enough. With his free hand he motioned us toward the tug. I guess it was about time to meet Dr. Obehail in person.

We cycled through the airlock and took off our helmets all the while the stranger kept his weapon on us. Dr. Obehail was there to greet us when the inner door opened.

"Ah, the famous Kingston child I've heard so much about. Harkinson, so nice of you to bring him to me, Valya awaits you both in the other room. Monuha, back outside as soon as you get them settled in nice and comfy." Then he turned and headed back to the tug's Control Room.

I looked at the suit that held the weapon. All he did was to motion us further down the corridor and into a small storeroom. Mom was sitting at a table going over some small shards of a glass-like substance. She didn't look up at first until dad spoke to her.

She jumped out of her chair and they hugged like they hadn't seen each other in a while. He whispered something in her ear and her eyes got really big. She quickly moved over to me and wrapped her arms around me.

"Oh my little boy, what ever has happened to you?" as she held me at arm's length and surveyed how tall I had gotten, I stood at least a couple of inches taller than her. "Oh my goodness how you've grown." She looked back at her husband and whispered, "How long has it been?"

"Mom, you can talk to me, I know you didn't really want to leave me there, but it's been almost five years since I landed on the planet."

"Five years? Oh, I can't believe it." she said. "Oh wait until Dora finds out."

I didn't say a thing about them, "But that also means that I'm now older than Arial." I added cheerily.

"I'm not sure how she'll take to that" mom replied skeptically, "She always liked to boss you around. They all missed you terribly while we were gone."

"I'm sure of that mom." I turned around to face the man in the suit. "OK, it's time to show yourself now."

But instead he tapped the door panel and stepped

back outside locking us in.

Mom and dad were talking quietly while I roamed around the room looking into this corner and that just hoping for something to use. I still had my sling-shot tucked away just in case.

"Jasom" mom called, "What do you know about the Haldon family?"

"Only the ones I've met, Arson, Jayla, Arial, and her sister Selda. Of course, now that I know who they are, I've also met Jared and his father Garlo who also went by the name of Hiram Wheeler."

I told them all about the people that I'd lived with and the people that I'd gotten to know. I mentioned that Garlo had hired a few thugs to ransack the farm, but they were now in custody, I didn't tell them how we had managed to overpower them, I didn't think mom could take the shock of what I'd been doing. Least of all, I didn't mention that Arial was with me and Dora and Tomer were back on Earth. The less they knew about them the better.

Things were quiet for several minutes; I was listening at the door when I heard the door unlatch and watched as the silent figure came back in again followed by Dr. Obehail, and he didn't look to happy.

"Problems doctor?" dad asked.

"Dr. LeOnard has not been able to open the main hatch. I think I should shoot someone."

"That won't solve anything" dad replied calmly.

"It would make me feel better though, I think I'll start with your wife."

I don't know what possessed me, "I can open it."

He turned to his silent partner with a smirk, "The Kingston brat thinks he knows how to open a door that's been sealed shut for several thousand years."

"I've just spent the last five years of my life living on the third planet. They have legends within their history that sound very much like this. I've studied about this and I think I know what it takes to unlock the door."

"Maybe I'll kill her anyway."

"And maybe you'll never get inside." I replied calmly. This was a dangerous game, playing against a mad man.

He studied my face for a while then nodded to the silent suit standing beside me.

I was dragged from the room and down the hall to the airlock. With our suits on we cycled through the airlock and out onto the tug's forward balcony where there was a line strung over to the derelict's side. I let the silent suit behind me furnish the propulsion, I couldn't tell if Dr. Obehail was behind us or not until we got to the hatch.

An intercom connection was attached to my suit and Obehail's voice simply said. "Open it, now!"

"Patience, I have to make sure this is the right hatch" as I shone a light all around the outer edges of the hatch. "Yes, there it is." Just a light scratching opposite the hinge.

I keyed my radio and spoke in English. "Alpha Hotel, proceed, confirming."

"What are you doing?" Dr. Obehail demanded.

"It's a sequence of commands" I replied hotly. "They have to be in order and timed properly."

"Juliet Kilo, proceed, confirmed" came the reply in Arial's voice, also in English. I smiled remembering how many times I had gone over these with her. It all had to be in English and I was hoping the good doctor didn't understand English.

"What crude language are you using anyway?" he demanded.

"Patience" I replied in Wessar, "It took years to learn this language and the commands."

"Ali Baba spoke thus!"

"Alpha Hotel responding, confirmed." She was in place and ready for the next step.

I have no idea why I happened to pick those next two words out of all of the fairy tales that I read, but they worked a miracle, the hatch popped open. I tried not to show my surprise.

CHAPTER 51

Obehail was so stunned that he didn't say a word. Slowly he regained his composure. "Monuha, open it up."

The silent figure beside me reached over and pulled the hatch wide open. As he did, the lights came on inside. "Kingston, you really amaze me. How did you know what it would take to open this door?"

I remained silent, both of them were so intent on what I had just done that they didn't see the baseball bat crash into Monuha's weapon. Somehow it fired and the projectile careened off the hull and punctured his suit.

Such a rapid decompression is messy; I was glad most of it was contained inside the suit. Obehail grabbed for the weapon, but he couldn't break Monuha's death grip. The projectile had only punctured the front of his suit, and the outpouring air pushed the body away from the derelict. Slowly, as it drifted further away it started to rotate and a yellowish substance began to emerge from the suit. Monuha was a Queryl!

I watched as Obehail wrestled with the suit still trying to free the weapon from its grasp as they disappeared between two small asteroids. What to do?

I keyed the radio, "Alpha Hotel, status?"

"I think we're all alone here" she replied as she hauled in her tie line, quickly coming to rest beside me.

"Nice job with the bat" I congratulated her after connecting the intercom again. "Where are the others? I haven't seen any of the other three scientists since we got here. You don't suppose that's he's killed them all off already?"

"Somebody should try to track him down; I don't feel safe with him still out here. And what was that yellowish stuff anyway?"

"Well it seems that we have another big mystery here" I replied, "Monuha is a Queryl. That's why he never took his suit off, they're Chlorine breathers."

She was silent for a bit. "We need to find out who's alive and who isn't, if you're right, we still have more people coming. And by the way, how did you open the hatch? Even Dr. LeOnard couldn't get it open?"

"Later." I had my suspicions, but we headed back to the tug. "Jayla? Mission complete. Execute lockdown"

"Jayla here, understood, he hasn't tripped the latch yet, but if someone doesn't show up soon to take him away, I might just trip the latch anyway."

"JK, understood, will send someone quickest. Be

vigilant, Obehail is still loose."

We returned to the tug as quick as we could and cycled through the airlock. The first thing I did was to let mom and dad out of the storeroom. I noticed a quick shock cross her face as she recognized who was with me. Dad was still digging in a pile of stuff and hadn't noticed.

"Harkinson dear?" she murmured to him as he finally pulled what he was looking for out of the pile. "What Valya?" As he slowly turned around to face us.

I'm not sure what was crossing his mind as Arial greeted them.

"How did you get here? You're supposed to be on the Quest with the rest of the children?" mom sputtered.

Arial spilled it all out in one big gasp of breath. "Dad dumped us on earth and we had to pull Jasom out of college to take care of us. Jasom's foster parents are taking care of Dora and Tomer, and we came back in the flyer."

"Where is everyone else" I demanded, "The only ones I've seen are Obehail and…Oh and by the way, Monuha is a Queryl and I think he's dead, but Obehail got away."

"That explains a lot" dad mused, "But opens up another mystery. How many on the council know about the Queryl? Obviously Dr. Obehail did, which means that it's a good bet that Councilor GraMorn does also. We need to find the others."

We started searching the tug, opening every door we could find, the tug was empty.

"Does the tug have a lock?" I asked, "I don't think we've seen the last of Obehail and I don't want him having access to the tug"

Dad was plotting something. "At least he can't get into the derelict."

"Uh, dad?" I mumbled.

"Yes son? What is it?" I watched the look on his face slowly change. "You didn't?" He exclaimed aghast. "How?"

"I have no idea really, I just used some old Earth fairy tale words and it just popped open." I didn't know what else to say.

"Can you relock it?"

"I'll try" and I rushed out of the room. Inside the airlock I slipped into my suit and hastily pulled myself across the line over to the derelict.

The hatch was still slightly open and the lights still on inside. I swung around and looked to see if I was alone and found Arial standing beside me. I hastily clipped the intercom on and told her to stand guard.

The hatch was heavy but I managed to keep my footing as I pushed it closed. I hated to close it because I didn't know if I could get it open again. With it shut tight I keyed the radio and issued the command to close as it told in the legend.

"Did it lock?" Arial prodded me and I pulled on the handle. It didn't open. "Good, let's get out of here."

We headed back along the line to the tug. Inside

mom and dad were suited and ready to leave. Outside I saw dad working on something with the latch to the main entry.

He motioned for us to follow him and we headed back toward the Tarkna.

The captain and Polland were still sitting quietly in the airlock we had tied them into. I confronted the captain first. "Monuha is dead; did you know he was a Queryl?"

The captain's face turned ashen. "That explains a lot. Polland, you've got a lot to answer for. What have you gotten us into?"

"It was nothing that you needed to know about, captain. And it's made you a lot of money in the meantime" Polland replied sourly. "You have no idea what you're up against Kingston, there are wheels within wheels going round and round."

"Captain" I remarked sarcastically, "I think that Polland has gone over the edge we should lock him up. Where's the brig?"

"Brigs full of scientists" he intoned in a dull monotone. "He was deep in thought and we left them there in the airlock while we went to rescue the scientists.

Near the rear of the ship we found the locked and barred door that held the brig. I unlocked the door and slowly they came out. Arson was the last one out, he had been captured by Monuha as he exited the airlock earlier.

Dad did introductions all around and we migrated

down to the rec room to talk. Most of them had only been in there since yesterday when Dr. LeOnard was locked up for failing to open the derelict; Arson had only been in there a few hours. He spent a moment talking with Jayla to make sure she was all right then he and Arial left to be with her.

Before she left Arial told me she'd only be a minute or two. I told her to be careful Obehail was still out there and we didn't know when our next guests would be arriving.

CHAPTER 52

Arson was about to cycle through the airlock when, "Tarkna come in. Councilor GraMorn here, come in."

"Arson, Arial, no!" I screamed, "Jayla, confirm exit, execute now, maximum propulsion."

"JK, confirm exit, executing now."

Baffled, Arson looked at me.

"Go get her" I told him, "I just told her to set the Quest on a random mission and to abandon ship. I told her to hide out beside our old friend Alpha-1, she'll need someone to help her get back here. Arial I'm going to need you here. We need to get everybody off this ship and into the derelict as fast as we can go. Let's go everyone!" as I followed Arial down the passage to the airlock where the captain and his chief were still bound to the exhaust valve.

It was not pretty; there was a look of utter terror on Polland's face and the despondent look on the captains made it look even sadder. We opened the door and hauled the two of them out of there and locked them in the brig.

"You lied to them about the airlock opening if they struggled didn't you?" Arial accused me as her parents cycled into the flyer hanger.

I just smiled and said "Of course. Remember Rawson?" We had a good laugh until Arson returned with Jayla in tow. I sensed that time was running out for us.

"OK people, let's get out of here" and we started cycling everyone through the airlock and into the flyer in the Tarkna's hanger bay. It was a tight fit but it was only going to be a short flight. I quickly moved the flyer away from the Tarkna and headed for the derelict.

We were almost there when the radio came alive. "Tarkna, we have you in sight, what is your status. Dr. Obehail what is your status?"

I heard a lurid reply of words and turned the receiver down; I had to concentrate as we approached the side of the derelict where I was sure the hanger bay was located. Dr. LeOnard was standing beside me and pointed out the tell-tale lights that had just come on. I keyed the radio and spoke the only thing I could think of, "Open Sesame".

The tell-tale lights blinked three times and a small door big enough to swallow the Tarkna opened in the side of the ship. I drove in and the door closed behind us. Slowly the lights came up enough to see where to dock the flyer. I did the best I could with an unfamiliar cradle landing and we all piled out and headed toward the door set in the nearest wall.

Over the door was a blinking red light. The light turned green and the door slid open. Inside the airlock was big enough for twice our number as we all filed in. Eerily the door silently closed behind us and the lighting got brighter just as the inner door opened.

Dr. LeOnard tapped me on the shoulder and when I turned around he had his helmet off and was sniffing the air; not that we had any choice in the matter at that point. "Not what I would call good air, it seems to be breathable but very very stale."

"Smells like a locker room" I remarked looking around, "where's the pile of sweaty underwear?" Dr. LeOnard sniffed again. "What's up doc?" I quipped, Arial laughed out loud and he got red in the face.

"I think that we should see how ready this ship is" as he started issuing orders to each of his colleagues.

Arson and Jayla headed for the rear of the ship as they were better at engineering while mom and dad set out for the piloting and command center which should be somewhere up front. That left Arial and I standing just inside the airlock staring at each other.

"Well, here's to you kid" I said. She gave me a funny look. "Let's check out the hanger bay and cargo hold. Maybe we'll find something useful." So we put our suits back on and went back into the hanger bay.

"You know, there's a lot of room in here. Not only is

the Tarkna's flyer in here but there are two others as well. I almost think I should go out and get my flyer and bring it in here as well."

"Oh no you don't, your father has instructed that we are to stay in here where it's safe. Besides, I want to see what's behind that hatch over there."

"Why not?" I replied. "Here let me see if I can figure out how to make the latch work."

"Sure thing genius. You can spend lots of time figuring it out, but let's just pull the handle and open the door. This is how it works. First you wrap your fingers around this little handle here and apply pressure to this spot and then you pull like this."

I gave her a skeptical look as she grabbed the door's handle and gave it a pull. Needless to say she gave me a knowing smirk as the door swung open freely.

Wow! This was a cargo hold and by the size of it just one of many. This one was nearly full of metal boxes and enigmatic machines all covered in a thin layer of dust. "Which one to look at first?"

"This is a job for Professor Whinoni" Arial remarked as she pawed through some filmy sheets laying on a table near the door. "The manifests should be here somewhere and then we'll have an idea of what they were hauling."

"Arial? Don't you at least want to see what's in one of these boxes?" I really just wanted to open stuff and gaze inside.

"And I thought you were the older and mature one? Can I pick which one?" she replied excitedly.

"Let's each pick one" as we turned around looking around and the multitude of possibilities. "I want that one!" we said in unison, both pointing at the same pile of boxes. Considering all of the boxes in here, it wasn't very large, but something about it called to me...well, to both of us I guess.

CHAPTER 53

We gazed at the top box. It was about four feet long, about one and a half wide, a foot thick, with writing on each side. I think it was the color that called me; it reminded me of army green camouflage. There were simple handles on the side and I picked it up and carried it over to the only raised surface in the hold which was against the front wall of the hold.

I shone my flashlight on the edges of the box looking for a latch and discovered that they were recessed on the back side. I had been reading the box upside down. I turned it around and pried the latches open and lifted the cover.

Now there was something that I recognized, the good old familiar form of a hunting rifle. It may have been a familiar form, but there were subtle differences between it and any hunting rifle I had ever seen. For one, the style was totally foreign and futuristic from an Earthly point of way. The rest of the container inside was filled with small boxes. "Whoa, and it comes with a stash of ammo as well. Nice!" as I reached in and pulled it out.

"Is that what I think it is?" Arial asked.

"Yup. The predecessors had weapons." I admired the weight and feel of it. It had a very nice balance not unlike the ones that Ned sold in his store. My finger fell on a slide catch and the empty clip fell out into my hand.

"Now's the time where you tell me that it wants you to load it, right?" Arial quipped.

"You read my mind Arial; open one of those little boxes."

She opened the first little box and dumped several cartridges into her palm and gave me a questioning look. "These little things?"

"Yup, they go into this clip like this" as I showed her how the clip worked. I was sure glad that Ned had insisted that I take a hunter safety course that first summer. He told me I couldn't work around firearms unless I knew how to safely handle both the gun and the ammo.

"Now I suppose you're going to start shooting at the walls?"

"Too dangerous, a bullet can ricochet off the walls and hit us. Safety rule, never load a firearm inside a building and always treat it as if it's loaded. No, I'm going to slip outside and do some target practice. Toss an empty container out and see if I can hit it."

"Well I better come along to make sure you don't

hurt yourself."

"Yes, you can try it out also. Dad, Arson, we're going to step outside on the hanger balcony and look around."

"OK kids. Radar doesn't show anything near us yet."

"He got the radar going?" Arial crowed.

"Yes, this ship appears to be fully functional. Have you found anything useful yet?"

"I'll let you know when we come back in."

CHAPTER 54

We'd found a couple of empty containers in a store-room earlier, one was made out of glass and I filled it up with water wildly anticipating what it would do when I shot it.

We stepped outside on the balcony and I clipped the intercom connection to her helmet. "Let's just toss this out slowly, too fast and it will get too far out to be seen."

I saved the glass bottle for later and pitched the empty ammo box out toward the open space above us where it wouldn't run into one of the asteroids. Too late I realized that it wouldn't show up in the dark and it quickly disappeared from sight.

"You need something that glows in the dark, like your flashlight" Arial told me through the intercom connection; we didn't want to broadcast so anyone could hear us outside.

I almost tossed my flashlight but instead gently pushed the glass jug of water out and away from us. "I have a better idea; train your flashlight on it."

It made an eerie glow as it slowly moved away from us. I kept it in my sights as long as I dared before pulling the trigger. I felt a slight momentary pressure against my shoulder and we saw a small reddish flash from the end of the barrel.

The jug exploded with a flare of glass and ice particles.

"Now what do I get to shoot at?" Arial wailed.

"Let's go find some more stuff to shoot at?" as we slipped back inside.

"Any more of those glass jugs?"

"No! That was the only one." and then from a container sitting on the floor inside the airlock, "Hey, how about a few of these thin skinned water bottles. They're not very big but they'll still hold water."

"They look good, how many of them are there?"

"Plenty, let's go" as we filled the little bottles and headed back outside.

After tossing and shooting about a dozen of them we decided to call it quits and head back inside.

"Arial, what's that light over there?"

The Tarkna was off to our left and the Quest was beyond it. This faint light was coming from the other direction. "I think we've got company, I don't know if they've seen us yet, looks like they're heading directly for the Tarkna.

We watched from our vantage point to see what this

new ship was going to do next. We didn't have long to wait as a beam of reddish orange light leaped out toward the Tarkna and destroyed it. There was a small fireball followed by pieces of wreckage flying away in all directions. There was another fireball as the beam licked out again this time destroying the King's Quest.

"Why have they done that?" Arial cried. "Who are these people?"

I raised the rifle and sighted on the aft propulsion unit. I had heard Charna once tell me that there was a small area of the propulsion unit that was highly susceptible to damage if it was struck by a projectile. The damage wouldn't be noticeable at first but the next time they used that propulsion unit it would malfunction and could possibly cause damage to the entire ship.

I had a nearly full clip left and just started pumping them into the aft propulsion unit. After all, I figured, it was just sitting there like a duck in the water.

"What are you doing?" Arial asked through the intercom connection, "You can't hurt a ship like that with just this little rifle."

I pulled the trigger until there was nothing left in the clip and stared at that ship willing it to blow up with a big bang. I did see a slight fizzle though. Maybe that was enough. "Let's get back inside; I think I damaged the propulsion unit. We don't want to be out here if it happens to go up with a big bang."

CHAPTER 55

We cycled back through the airlock and hung our suits before heading up front to the command center to see what was going on.

"Where have you two been?" Dad screamed at me, "We've been trying to call you for twenty minutes." He slowly calmed down as Arson put a hand on his shoulder.

"Calm down Harkinson, I'm sure these two have been behaving themselves." And then he intentionally gave me a cold stare. "Haven't you?"

"Cool it dad" Arial confronted him, "we've been target practicing out on the hangar balcony. We turned off our radios so you wouldn't hear what we were doing. Not that I'd let you listen in if we were."

I understood that the last was an act of defiance on her part.

"Dad, we found a cargo hold and decided to open just one little Christmas present."

"You what?" he replied in a bewildered tone.

"Sorry about the Earth reference, but that's not my fault." I replied cryptically. "We were watching while that ship destroyed the Tarkna and then the King's Quest. I was so mad at them I emptied the clip into the rear propulsion unit." Then with probably a little too much enthusiasm and a little bit of glee, "and I hit it too."

"You were throwing bottles at the other ship? Just what are you talking about Jasom?" then mom turned on Arson. "Arson, I should never have let you talk me into leaving him on that dreadful planet."

"No mom, we were shooting at the bottles that we filled with water. When the bullet goes through the bottle the water spurts out into ice crystals. Very harmless, and I'm a better shot than Arial is." I announced with pride.

"I let you win!" she added sullenly.

Mom looked from one of us to the other. "I don't know what to believe."

"It's nice to have bewildered parents" I said as they wondered what I was talking about.

"Dad" I asked quietly, "What happens when a propulsion unit has a small internal malfunction that doesn't show on the control panel?"

"What kind of malfunction are you talking about?" he replied with a hint of interest.

"Well Charna once told me that all propulsion units have a small vulnerability when they are powered down. If a fast moving missile happens to enter into the chamber and hit a certain weak spot it will cause a rupture that is not readily apparent to the operator."

"And when it is powered up it could cause damage to the engine" he finished for me. "And you have done such damage to this other ship?"

"I believe so, I think one of my bullets must have hit something; there was a little fizzle of light showing inside the chamber. If we could only get them to power it up they could damage the engine enough to disable their ship."

"Hmmm!" he was thinking about it, when I had a bright idea.

"How about if we take this ship and move away from them? Hey Dr. LeOnard, are the engines working? Can we get underway?"

"Maybe later young man, I'm working on something else right now." He had his head buried in an open access panel. "Need to make sure the air cleaners are working, wait! There they go."

I started to feel air moving, it even smelled better. "Good work Doctor, that's much better." Sarcastically I added, "But if we don't start getting this hunk of junk moving they're going to blow us out of existence, good air or bad air."

Suddenly the radio came to life. "Hey there! You people hiding on the derelict. You're trespassing. Remove yourselves immediately."

Dad stepped up to the radio. "And where do you

suppose we should go? You've already destroyed both of our ships?"

"The Tarkna belonged to me and has served its usefulness. The other fired on us and we defended ourselves."

"The other ship was mine" Dad responded, "And was unarmed. It was maliciously destroyed and for that we demand recompense."

"I take it that I'm speaking with Harkinson Kingston then. You and your family are under arrest along with the Haldon and Janon families."

"And I know who you are too, Councilor GraMorn. You are a Renegade, traitor, and a murderer. Through your actions a young boy has lost his parents and several other families have been torn apart. You will surrender to the nearest federal official to be returned to Evenset for trial."

All the while they were verbally sparring; Dr. LeOnard and I were hastily working on getting the engines going. Professor Whinoni was interpreting the writings on the screens and was activating them almost as fast as we got them running.

"Which ones are the pilot's chairs?" She pointed to the two fronts seats flanking what was probably the captain's chair. "Arial! Grab the other one."

She gave us a quick rundown on what she thought was each control. I quizzed her on one as it didn't feel right. She quickly read the label again and agreed with me. "Sometimes one of their words has more than one meaning. Makes the interpretation a little difficult at times, and this is the first time I've had to do it under duress."

"I'll handle it from here. Arial bring the right flank up to twelve percent, I think that's about what it will take for threshold movement." Threshold movement is the amount of power it takes to begin movement. I was guessing that it wouldn't be much more than that.

A quick glance at Arial's board and we were ready. "Keep a close eye on the councilor's ship. The quicker we get moving the less likely they are to find out they have propulsion problems. An indicator on my board began to rise. "We're moving people, you'd better be strapped down." I hollered. I couldn't take the time to look.

"I'll keep an eye on the other ship" Arson spoke from behind us, he was sitting in the captain's chair. "Where was the atomic cannon located Jasom? I don't see any indication of it from here."

"It came out from under the nose cone; I could see it when they destroyed the Tarkna. I don't know if it swivels. Arial, be ready to up to twenty five percent on your side, then let me have control of both sides. I'm going tangent to them so they can't track us with their cannon."

The derelict was beginning to respond to the controls but sluggishly. I needed more power. "Power setting to fifty percent, confirm."

"Power settings to fifty percent, confirmed." she replied.

That felt much better, still not as nimble as the flyer, but there was a ton of power under this hood. "Hang on crew, here we go" as I twisted both controls simultaneously. The derelict responded slowly at first but built up speed as the engines roared to life. We were rotating up and out of the asteroid field and into open space. We'd still be sitting ducks if they ever got turned around to face us so I dropped us below the ecliptic and down under the other side of the asteroid field. Without going back into the field we were still sitting ducks.

"It's no shame to cut and run son." dad called from one of the stations behind us.

"I know dad, but I was hoping for a miracle."

"Arial, Jasom, prepare for full power on my command." Arson was making the decision to run.

"Where to, captain?" I asked.

"LeOnard? Do we have navigation yet?"

"Coming captain" he was beginning to breathe hard, I think the strain was getting to him. "Almost there."

I could hear him conferring with the professor Whinoni on something. Behind us I could see the Renland Commander slowly drifting into view.

"Got it" LeOnard crowed. "Where we headed captain?"

"Just point us toward Evenset, that's where he's expecting us to go."

"That will take us very close to this system's star,

we'll have to offset jump part way and correct from there."

"Just point us in that direction then drop us near the third planet. Got it?"

"You're the captain."

"Let's see if your theory is going to work Jasom. We're going to stress both of his propulsion units. Jasom, on my mark!"

"Yes captain, on your mark, ready." I replied.

"Mark!" He called.

"Mark, confirmed, full power on course, engaged."

CHAPTER 56

Whoa, this buggy had some serious horses under the hood. I've punched the flyer before, but this guy shoved me back in my seat so hard my lips were curled back over my cheeks.

And then, it all stopped and returned to normal. I looked over at Arial and she was as white as a sheet. I quickly switched my screens to rear view. It was nearly ten minutes before we began to see the lights on the Renland Commander slowly closing down on us. The rear propulsion unit had a strange glow to it.

The radio beeped again and Councilors GraMorn's voice came on. "Enough of this!" he screamed, "Surrender at once or be destroy…"

The radio went silent as the Renland Commander slowly erupted in an enormous fireball starting with the rear propulsion unit. Without waiting for the command I quickly pushed us further away from the carnage.

We sat in silence as the afterimage slowly faded

from sight. Nobody felt like saying anything but we still had things to do.

"Jasom" mom called from the doorway, "I think you may have used too much acceleration, Dr. Heinchi has passed out, Jayla's tending to him now. Have we gotten away from councilor GraMorn? That awful man, wait until I get back to the council. I'll have him arrested for what he's done." Mom was really upset. I'll let dad take care of that.

"Well captain, what do we do now?"

Arson just sat there looking at the screens with a soft smile on his face. "I like this ship! I really, really, like this ship." Well, after all it was several sizes bigger than the Quest had been. "What do you think?" as he smiled at me. "This one will hold more families, don't you think."

I could see Arial's face turn red, I knew what she was thinking, but I still had other things I needed to do first. "I need my flyer first, can we go back for it now?"

"Sure Jasom."

"And a little slower this time?" Arial piped in, "I don't like people seeing my teeth sticking out like that." She cast a quick smile over at me which I returned. If we'd been closer I might have taken her hand, but I wanted my flyer back first. The rest can wait till later on.

CHAPTER 57

We now know that the name of this ship is the "Cornish Talisman", a name similar to several others of the derelict ships that could be determined. No other ship so far had been in this usable a shape, this could very well be the last of their ships.

Prof. Whinoni had started to decipher the ships log. From it we learned that at some ancient time they had landed on the third planet of this system and started a colony on one of the major landmasses. The description given did not match any of the present day continents so there was no way to determine where they actually landed.

They had landed not once, but several times, bringing in more colonists each time. It wasn't until after the last landing that the ship was moved out here and programmed to hide amongst the slowly moving asteroids. It was able to absorb enough energy from the wan sunlight to maintain its cover.

That was over ten thousand years ago as best she

could determine. From what we knew about them, this time period lined up with the last known sightings of them anywhere in the explored vastness; at least that we know of to this day.

"There's something that we must do before we can go back to Evenset." Arson announced. "We know that my estranged brother in law has been living on this planet Earth, and is preparing to cause havoc among the natives. I need to take him back for trial. We have observers stationed in many places and they have kept me up to date on his doings. It is up to me to bring him in."

"And you're not going alone" I chimed in, "I have unfinished business as well and mom and dad want their daughter back.

"What about poor Tomer?" Arial asked.

"They didn't have any family that I know of" dad said, "He is truly an orphan."

"Valya, do you think you and Jayla can run this ship while a couple of us go visiting?"

"Arson, why don't we just park this buggy on the back side of the moon and take two flyers down?" I glanced at Arial and she smiled back at me. "You take the Tarkna's flyer and Arial and I will take mine. Just follow us down; I've learned a few tricks since you guys left me here five years ago."

Grudgingly, we moved the ship out of orbit and over behind Earth's single moon.

Dr. LeOnard said they had plenty to keep busy with and hoped to have most of the other systems mapped out. "You should have a fully functional ship ready for you on your return Captain Arson."

"Very well doctor. You know how to get in touch with me if you need anything."

"I don't anticipate anything out of the ordinary captain…and, if you don't mind, would you bring back some fresh fruit?"

"Of course doctor, fresh fruit it is."

We gathered out in the hanger, Arson and Jayla would be taking mom and dad with them. Jayla gave me a sly look and a nod as Arial and I climbed into my flyer and slid out of the hanger bay. They followed us down about the same way I did those many years ago and landed gently in the front driveway of the farm.

Fortunately it was late at night and the Farnham's children were all in bed. The porch light came on and I saw Ted Farnham standing in the doorway.

"Good evening Ted, it's me, Jasom Kingston. We're back."

CHAPTER 58

As soon as the hulls on our flyers had cooled enough from our descent through the atmosphere, I backed my flyer into the same bay that it had sat in for so long before. Arson just moved his into the main opening in the barn. With so many people around I didn't think that we needed to worry about anyone stumbling onto them.

I introduced everyone and asked him about Ned and Henrietta and the children.

"They're doing well, moved across the street to the larger house and found a tenant for our old place. I'm glad you let us rent this place; we really needed the room for the kids. But where's my manners, come inside before you freeze to death, the temperature will be dropping into the twenty's tonight.

I sniffed loudly, "smells like a storm coming in too, feels like we could get some snow tonight. Have you heard a forecast Ted?"

"It's going to be a big one; they've already had to

close Route 2 out beyond Chinock. Hasn't been too bad around here yet though. Are you guys staying long?"

We settled around the kitchen table while Martha made coffee. I had gotten used to the smell as Henrietta made a fresh pot every morning but wouldn't let me have any until I was eighteen; something about it was supposed to stunt your growth.

She set cups down in front of all of us and I watched in amusement as Arial carefully sniffed the hot vapors from the steaming cup.

Arson on the other hand, "Oh man have I missed the smell of fresh brew!" As he carefully sipped at the hot liquid in his cup. "Ummm!"

"Be careful Arial, it's supposed to stunt your growth. At least that's what they used to tell me."

The laughter was quite welcome after the last few days of stress. "Days?" I thought. "Ted, what's today? How long have we been gone?"

He gave me a light chuckle in response. "You left the day before yesterday, maybe about 72 hours, tops. How long did you think you were gone?"

"It felt like an eternity." In the background I could hear a clock ticking. "Then today is what, Friday?"

"It will be in the morning, we just put the kids to bed."

"And it's getting late. May I use your phone?" He nodded and I called Ned.

CHAPTER 59

Ned came out and drove us all back to their new place with more introductions and reunions between a sleepy Dora and mom and dad. This late at night Tomer was fast asleep and we decided not to wake him. We took turns telling the story and I learned more of what had happened before Arial had arrived in my dorm room.

But time was still ticking right along and I noticed that Dora was curled up on the couch next to mom and they were both fast asleep. Dad's eyes were blinking and Arson looked like his face was glazed. Jayla's face looked like a frozen mask and her eyes were wide open; too much caffeine I guess.

Arial was sitting beside me, her eyes were closed and she was gently, but slowly, leaning forward. I put my arm around her and she snuggled against my shoulder and started snoring softly in my ear; just enough to keep me awake.

"I think we have some very tired guests here Henrietta. Would you get me the keys to your old place and we'll see if we can get some of them settled up there."

Dad picked up Dora and put her back in her bed while Ned unfolded the hide-a-bed for him and mom. Ned led Arson and Jayla, while I helped Arial across the street and up the stairs.

Ned and Henrietta had moved into Hiram's old place and fortunately it came fully furnished. They hadn't had to move a lot of furniture so both bedrooms still had beds. There weren't any sheets, but Ned had brought plenty of blankets.

Arial took my old bed and I dug out the sleeping bag from the corner where I had rolled it up just a few days ago. I told Ned that we really appreciated their hospitality as I curled up on the floor and fell instantly asleep. "When had I slept last?" was the last thing I remember thinking.

CHAPTER 60

"Hey, kid! Wake up! Hiram wants to see you." Groggily I rolled over and whacked my head on front leg of the stand in the corner of the living room. Then I came fully awake expecting to see Hawthorne sitting there. What I didn't expect to see was Arial smiling back at me.

"Hey there sleepy head, dad wants us all together ASAP, brother dear." My gaze traveled up and around to see Dora staring back at me.

My mind was full of cobwebs as I growled back at her. "Arial, will you tell this little twerp what I'm like when I don't get enough sleep?"

Dora's eyes lit up as she bounced off the couch and out the door.

"I better reinterpret what you just told her before the mothers get the wrong idea" as she slowly got up from the chair and followed Dora.

"Rats. I wonder if I can stick my other foot in my mouth."

Painfully I washed up realizing that I was all alone up here. We had taken turns sleeping on the way out, and yes there had been just the two of us and there wasn't any way that Arial would have stayed behind; and the way things turned out I'm glad she had.

"Jasom?" a querulous little voice called.

Now I know I'm in trouble, they sent Tomer over to get me. "Just washing up Tomer. How are you this morning?" I asked him as he stared up at me.

"How did you get so big?" he said in wonderment.

"We'll have to sit down some time and I'll tell you all about it. How would that be?"

"I'd like that. Is it all right if I play with some of your toys?"

"Anything you want Tomer. And, I actually have a few you haven't seen yet. Wait until later and I'll dig out the good ones." I was happy to see his face brighten up.

I smiled at him as I wondered what was going to happen to him. He was another orphan just like I had been. Actually no, I had been sure that they would come back for me. Poor little Tomer didn't have any family to come back for him.

As we strolled back across the road I told him that I knew several boys his age that lived right near here and I'd see if he could play with them after breakfast. I kept my promise and a few hours later he was having fun playing with little Tommy, Holly's youngest brother who was also

8 years old. Billy brought him over along with his other sister Sally who was eleven years old and just as precocious as her older sister. He stayed to talk with us while all of our parents caught up on other matters.

The old folks were so wrapped up in what they were talking about that they completely ignored us. "Come on guys" I said, "let's go over to the playground." then I remembered that it was Friday. "Hey why aren't you guys in school?"

"It's a holiday Jason, you forgotten already?"

"Sorry, been so busy lately I've lost all track of time."

"When are you leaving Jason?" Billy asked as we watched the younger ones playing at the schools playground.

"I haven't stopped long enough to figure that out" I told him. "This last week was just a big blur."

Then he turned his attention to Arial. "Are you going back where you came from? Funny you've never told me where that is." She just smiled sadly back at him.

He was fishing I knew, but Billy was only seventeen and had to finish high school and then college. I knew how to handle this.

"Where are you planning on going to college Billy? I thought you were interested in Physics or was it Chemistry?" Arial wandered over to where the girls were swinging.

"Well, I was thinking my best bet would probably

be right here in state, but the absolute best would be back east. I'd really like to get into M.I.T."

"I've heard of M.I.T., didn't think it suited me. Now I've got to determine if I should go back or not?" I really needed to take the time to sit down and talk it over with mom and dad.

They'd lost their ship which had been their home for almost twenty years. Maybe he and Arson could make a go of it with the Cornish Talisman. There would be a squabble about ownership from the council and I'm sure there were going to be other problems with regard to Dr. Obehail and councilor GraMorn, and more especially their association with the Queryl. Those things didn't seem relevant to me right now, I needed to focus on what mattered the most to me.

My gaze drifted across the playground to where Arial was swinging beside Dora. Sally was pushing Dora, but Arial was having trouble getting it to go.

"I don't have a chance with her do I?" Billy broke into my reverie.

"I think you have plenty of time to find the right one for you. And sometimes it may just be someone that you've known for a long time and just never thought of her in that way." I clapped him on the shoulder. "Billy, I really appreciate what you did for us last weekend. I didn't realize that it would be that dangerous and I'm sorry for that. You didn't get in to much trouble for us did you?"

"Nah, mom never suspected a thing and when Mrs. Johnson came over with the other two kids she forgot all about it."

"I doubt that. Mothers don't forget about things like that. If she ever found out what had really happened... Whoa, I hate to think about what she would have done to me."

Billy laughed. "She'd probably have made you marry Holly."

I gave him a pained look and we both had a good laugh.

"Got to take the kids home" He told me checking his watch, "time for lunch. Sally! Tommy! Time to go home." He gathered them together and they all waved goodbye as they left the playground. We didn't have to be back for another hour and I was going to stay out here as long as I could. Might as well start with Arial.

"OK Arial, first lesson." And I showed her how to work the swing by swinging your body forward and back at just the right time. Dora was a quick learner and was already swinging up quite high. "No higher Dora" I called, "there's a point where it gets very dangerous and you could fall off and hurt yourself." Tomer was doing pretty good by himself too.

Arial was still having trouble so I pulled her back and gave her a shove. Out and back she went. "That's fun" she said, "Higher!" So I pushed a little harder this time and stepped back just a little so I could reach higher. She swung back up higher than before and I reached up and gave it all I had.

Well, she was a little heavier than Dora, more mass takes more work to move, and I knew better than to say it outright that way. I had learned about talking about weight and girls in the same sentence in high school with very bad results.

"Jasom!" Tomer screamed, "look at me" as he swung up almost as high as Dora.

I felt the breeze of the swing go by as Arial came back and went up over my head. I had stepped back so that I wouldn't get hit in the head if I was distracted. What I didn't expect was that she had tucked her legs under her on the way back instead of out straight.

One foot on each shoulder was enough to pick me up off my feet and toss me backwards into the grass. "Ohhh!" was all I could say as three concerned faces stared down at me.

"Jasom!" Tomer cried, "I didn't know you could fly!"

"And backwards too." Dora chimed in. "Are you OK?"

Arial hadn't said a word. Slowly she knelt down by my side. "Do you hurt anywhere?"

I untensed my muscles and slowly flexed. So far so good. Then I felt her fingers going over my legs. "Can you feel that?" she asked.

"I think everything is where it belongs. Is there anything sticking out where it's not supposed to?"

Again her fingers running across my arms, "yeah, all good there." It didn't seem to hurt, yet.

"OK, now gently try to roll over." She gave me a concerned look as I slowly rolled over.

That worked, and I slowly climbed to my feet. I would be sore tomorrow.

"Let's head back for lunch." I told them as Arial helped me to walk off the playground and out to the street. Ned's car was sitting by the curb and he was standing there waiting for us.

He just shook his head at the bunch of us as I stumbled to the car. "You go off for a week to save the world without a scratch and less than a day later you get injured on a children's toy." He slowly shook his head. "And here I thought we brought you up better than that?" He was almost laughing by that time.

"Haw, haw, haw" then, "Ow, ow, ow." I didn't need to laugh right now, it hurt too much but I would survive. I also had decided what I wanted to do and now I had to see what the rest of the families thought about it.

CHAPTER 61

After lunch we all gathered around the table. It was a tight fit as Ned's table only had enough chairs for six. Arial sat on a stool between her parents and Dora and I sat beside mom and dad on the other side of the table almost into the living room where Tomer was playing with some of the toys I had dug out of the back of my old closet. He had never seen cowboys and Indian action figures before.

As the host, Ned started off. "I take it that since your home has been destroyed by the evil councilor GraMorn that you intent to take over the Cornish Talisman as your own?"

"That's a rather interesting way of putting it Ned" dad said, "But nonetheless accurate. The Haldon's and Kingston's have decided that we have earned the use of it even though the council will not agree with us, and they will probably try to take it away from us."

"And just how do you propose to keep it? Won't you need some sort of proof of ownership?" He let that sink in. "It appears to me, from what you've told me so far, that the owners of that ship actually settled this planet, don't you think that it would belong to them?"

Arson had a grim set to his face, "Under who's laws of ownership shall it be decided then, Earth's or the council's? After all, it was abandoned countless centuries ago and it seems there's no one left to claim ownership."

"An abandoned ship, just a few millions of miles from this planet just sitting there waiting for someone to come back for it." Ned continued; I was beginning to wonder where he was going with this.

"What are you driving at Ned?" Arson demanded hotly. "Our ship has been destroyed by this idiotic council of morons and we're haggling about who owns it? Seems to me that whoever opens it first should be the owner. Don't you agree?"

"And doctor Obehail, spent months working at it." I added.

"And did he get it open?" Ned persisted.

There was no response from either of us, the question just hung there in the air between us as if it were a blinking neon sign.

"Precisely my dear captain, precisely!" Ned continued. "And just who was the one who opened it?"

Arson was about to raise his voice when it dawned on him. Everyone slowly turned to face me. Slowly it also dawned on me what they were talking about.

Ned came to my rescue. "You see my dear Captain, we've now correctly identified who has salvage rights to the Cornish Talisman. Not only did he discover it, but he was also the first one to enter it. I think that that is more than enough to establish ownership, wouldn't you agree?"

"Oh my word Jason" Henrietta remarked, "You're not only a landlord, but now you own a spaceship as well." She turned to Ned. "Nedwick! How can we make sure that all of this is legal? From what I'm hearing, the very council that we work for has been infiltrated by everything that we've been working to prevent." She was very upset.

"But there is also another person to consider here." Ned continued soberly.

Henrietta gave him a quizzical look.

"Ned means" I told her, "what are we going to do with Tomer. He has no family left."

Soberly she considered the situation, "Why we're not too old to take another orphan in" she replied, "and we did alright with you, didn't we?"

"Perhaps we should ask the others before assuming anything" I sighed, "and find out what Tomer wants."

I looked over at Arson. "Well captain? What do you have to say?"

"Jasom, I'm a captain without a ship what do you want me to say?"

"We'll deal with the ship part later, Tomer comes first? You and Jayla have raised two children and mom and dad have raised two children. What's in your future now? Do you have a plan that would include taking a young child along?" I had a plan and I didn't think they were going to like it.

"What future do we have without a ship?" he replied eyes downcast. "I might just as well start farming." Then a sobering thought occurred to him. "And I can't even do that, I signed over that property to you as well."

"And I've rented that property out and made enough money to fund my way through college. I appreciate what you gave to me even though it was probably the darkest two weeks of my life." I told them a few things about how I survived until Mr. Dressler and Mrs. Martin found me. Mom was almost to tears.

"But I'm not going to dwell on that. I have a job for you captain, if you're willing to accept it." I noticed dad's head perk up. "And yes, dad, it includes you and mom too."

Dad had been listening closely and I saw a look on his face that he had an idea where I was headed. But he didn't know all of it.

"All right Jasom, I'm up for it, just what do you want us to do?" Arson replied.

"As rightful owner of the Cornish Talisman, according to Earth law" Ned nodded when I looked to him for confirmation, "I need a captain and crew to man my ship and return the scientists to the world of their choice."

Dad was whispering to mom and I could see her face turn slightly white. Jayla still hadn't caught up with what was going on, but for her and Arson it wouldn't be as much of a shock.

"And what if they don't want to go back? What if they want to stay and study the ship?" Arson asked.

"If that is their choice, then it's up to you to decide whether they are worthy to become crew members. The Kingstons and Haldons will decide who is to stay on as crew. Can I put my trust in you four to do that?"

They looked at each other and all nodded acceptance.

"Then, Captain Arson Haldon, assume your command. I would advise you to make contact with those scientists immediately and assess the situation and report back to me at your earliest convenience."

"Aye, aye, Admiral Kingston!" He replied with a salute and a broad smile.

I smiled back, "Carry on captain." I then turned to the others. Mom seemed resolute. "Dora?"

"Yes Admiral?" she replied brightly.

"I know this is a pretty big question for you, but…"

"Jasom, my older but dumber brother, of course I'll stay here with Tomer. He needs me and I really like it here." Then she turned to Henrietta, "Is it all right with you if both of us stay here with you and Ned? Pretty please? Mom! Can I? I'll be bored to tears without anyone else to play with."

"Mom, Dad? As you may already have figured out, I have decided to stay here and I think for the next few years you guys are going to be very busy. We will expect you to drop in often. This ship I'm entrusting to you guys is very fast. I hate to turn it over to Arson, but I'm not ready for it and I can't think of anyone else I would rather trust it with." I watched the tears roll down her cheeks and the sudden dawning in Jayla's eyes as she realized what mom was just realizing. They hugged each other.

"Son" dad said, "It's every parents dream, and dread, to turn their child loose. You're mother and I have noticed that you've really grown up and matured. My thanks to you, Ned and Henrietta for all you've done for him."

There was nothing I could say to that and it was hard to keep the tears from flowing. I hugged both of them.

Only one person left, Arial. The girl I had adored for so many years. She had been a pain; older, lofty, and bossy when we were younger. We had been through a lot over the last week and it had been like something totally new for us. I had felt closer and more equal to her than ever before.

"Admiral Kingston?"

"Umm, yes captain? What can I do for you?" I hadn't quite figured out how to ask her what she wanted to do.

"I'd already given my permission when I left her with you last week. The rest is up to the two of you."

Both Arson and Jayla smiled at me, but where was Arial? I looked around the room and noticed that not only had Dora and Tomer disappeared, but Arial had gone with them.

Arson clapped me on the shoulder. "We can finish up here, why don't you go talk to her. And be gentle."

"Henrietta, would you get in touch with Mrs. Martin? See if she can come over now?" I needed to speak with her anyway and maybe she could help out with Arial.

She smiled back at me, "Of course dear, I told her we might need her and she's just waiting for me to call her back."

"Thank you. We may be a while." And I left the room in search of my fellow castaways.

I finally found them back at the playground. Billy had brought Sally and Tommy to play with Tomer and Dora. At the moment he was having a very animated conversation with Arial. Instead of butting in I let them talk while I wandered around the school yard.

CHAPTER 62

I was deeply lost in thought when a familiar voice brought me back to reality.

"Hello Jason, it's good to see you again."

"Nice to see you again too Mrs. Martin, how have you been?" as I turned and greeted her cordially.

"I see that you have found your family. Does that mean you're not an orphan anymore?" We turned and looked back at the others. "She's pretty, your sister?"

"The little one is, her name is Dora. I think you'll be seeing a little more of her from now on. The little boy is Tomer and both of his parents were killed recently. He was their only child and there is no family that we know of. Ned and Henrietta will be taking both of them in. I was hoping you would be able to smooth the way for them."

"I would be glad to. What about your parents, have you found out anything about them?"

"Oh, yes, would you like to meet them? They will be leaving soon, matters of state is about the best way I can describe it."

"And?' she prompted, nodding toward Arial.

I blushed a little. "That's Arial, and it's complicated."

"I see" she said with a mischievous smile. "How can I help?"

I explained the best way I knew how, the complicated relationship between us and how I didn't know what to do for her. I didn't want to lose her again, but I wanted to finish college and she needed something to do. "Do you and your brother think you could come up with some program like the one you did for me? I want her to have the same opportunities that I had while she is staying here. She's very hands on, I guess you could say."

"Well, I think you've given me quite a challenge." She seemed intrigued by the idea. "Would you mind introducing us?"

"My pleasure" I replied as I took her over to where Arial was talking with Billy.

The two of them walked away as I stood there with Billy.

"I still don't have a chance, do I?" he asked.

I smiled back at him. "No, I don't think so."

"Where did you guys go anyway, I went over to see you the day after you know what happened, and Ned told me that you and Arial had gone off together and it may be several days before you came back. I thought you guys had run off to get married."

I had a good laugh for a minute, poor Billy. "And that would be bad? Billy, I've known Arial for many years, since we were both quite young. Our families have traveled together ever since then."

"So you two are not romantically involved?"

I didn't say anything as I looked over at Arial talking with Mrs. Martin. Just how did I feel about her? Perhaps living so close together for so long isn't such a good start for a lifelong relationship.

"Billy, I'm not sure what our relationship is. I know there's friendship, comradeship, and that I've adored her for as long as I can remember. But we have been apart for several years now and it's almost as if we're starting all over again, almost like we are meeting for the first time again."

"Wow, maybe there is something to that old saying."

"What saying is that Billy?" I inquired?

"That absence makes the heart grow fonder. I know I've grown fonder just in this last week" as he smiled at me.

I hung my head in thought, she and I needed to talk, and soon. I knew what I wanted to do. Just about then Arial waved goodbye to Mrs. Martin and walked slowly back to where Billy and I stood watching the kids play on the swing set.

CHAPTER 63

I checked my watch and decided it was time to head back to the house for supper, besides it was beginning to get colder out.

"OK kids, time to go home. You guys can get together again tomorrow and the next day after that."

I said goodbye to Billy as Arial and I herded the kids back toward the house.

"Well, how do you like Mrs. Martin?" I asked her. "She was a big help to me when she found me all alone out at the farm. Since then she and her brother have been a big help in my fitting in around here as well as getting into a great university."

She didn't say anything and I began to wonder what was bothering her. I put my hand on her shoulder and we turned to face each other. A person's face can say a lot, and I knew she was trying to come to grips with what she wanted to do. I could imagine that she wouldn't have the same opportunities that I had had because of her age.

She gave me a wan smile and we continued on in silence. At the railroad crossing the lights started flashing as it was time for the afternoon freight to pass through. I told the children to stand back with us and watch the train go by.

Neither one of them were afraid and were thrilled as the whistle wailed and the train approached from the west and the sound trailed off as it disappeared into the southeast and out of sight. I was heartened to see that Tomer was excited about seeing it and Dora was also, but she kept her excitement in check. She was fitting into her "big sister" role quite well.

Back at the house the big pow-wow had been replaced by the smells of food cooking. The three women were in the kitchen talking quite animatedly about food preparation, but Ned, Arson, and dad were not around.

Henrietta told me they had gone over to the garage to look at his automobile. I guess I was going alone as Arial joined the kitchen crew and Dora and Tomer headed into the bedroom to play.

I wandered over to the garage and was surprised to see Arson trying to figure out how to ride my bicycle and dad had his head under the hood of the car with Ned. I felt like a fifth wheel without a car.

"Jasom?"

"Yes captain?"

"Are you sure that anyone can learn to ride this stupid thing?"

"It's all balance. Here let me show you." I jumped on and rode it down to the corner and back. Just for fun I came back full speed and drifted the rear tire spraying gravel as I came to a stop heading back the way I had come from. "See, piece of cake."

He just stood there shaking his head with a smile. "Maybe I'm just too old to learn. Got a moment?"

"Sure, what's on your mind?" I suspected that I was in for the father of the daughter speech.

We walked down the road toward the highway and the turn out to the farm.

"Do you remember the message that I sent you right after I left Arial and the children with you?"

I nodded and wondered what was on his mind.

"When I wrote that I didn't expect to be seeing any of you again. I was giving you my daughter to take care of without her consent."

"Yes, I remember. But you should also realize that she read it at the same time I did. I think she understood what you were doing and why."

"Well, things have worked out much better than I thought they would, and now I wonder if it was such a good idea." He sounded a little nervous.

I smiled grimly back at him. "You did what you thought at the time was the best thing for the children; Arial included." I paused for a moment in thought. "Have you spoken with Arial about this? It seems to me that you should square things with her first." Man I was beginning to sound like the father here.

"I suppose that I should. I've always thought that you two would make a good couple but maybe I was wrong about that?" He sounded a little guilty about that admission.

"And I'm sure you'd make a great father-in-law as well, but I don't think that either one of us are quite ready for that just yet. Why don't we just let time decide, shall we?" We shook hands and started back to the house.

Surprisingly, when we got back, dad and Ned were still in the garage. Arson took one more look at the bicycle then shook his head and wheeled it back into the garage.

Regretfully I didn't feel like talking with them and stood out by the road and stared at the sun setting in the west lost in thought.

"It really is beautiful around here, isn't it?" Arial spoke from beside me. "Everything seems so fresh and different then what we grew up with. Why is that?"

"Because, my dear Arial" I replied still looking at the sunset, "no matter how you disguise the smell, the air in a ship is recycled. It's used, then used again, and finally used up."

"You are so hard to understand some times" she said sarcastically.

"I think that I've been very lucky to have spent the

last few years here on this planet. And I also think that the inhabitants of this planet are the descendants of the Predecessors."

She smiled at me and said in a soft voice, "You like it here, don't you?"

I felt refreshed. "Yes I do. How would you like to share it with me?"

The look of fright on her face was all I needed for an answer. "That's what I thought" as I smiled at her.

"I don't' understand, what do you mean?" she asked quizzically.

"It means that I think you would tolerate living here with me, but wouldn't be happy living here." I gave her a wan smile. "I guess I've known it for a while now."

We walked further on watching the sunset before us. "What did Mrs. Martin tell you?"

"She told me how she had helped you to become 'assimilated' into the local culture. I guess she thought she could do the same for me, but the more she talked about it the less comfortable I felt with it. It didn't feel right for me somehow."

I could see that the last part had been hard to admit. "What did you tell her? Mrs. Martin is a very nice person and I think she would do whatever she told you she would."

"I told her I'd think about it, but I could see that she knew what I was going to do. I just wish I knew" she continued bitterly.

"So then, I guess you need something that 'feels right' for you then?"

"You're not proposing…"

"That's not the right word to use" I chuckled. "Around here, proposing means marriage and I know you've already ruled that out for our immediate futures."

I could see her face burning in the dimming light. "OK" she said, "but I'm still not sure what I really want to do yet. But I sense that you have an idea that I might like?"

"Nothing personal yet." I let her stew with that remark; I wanted to make sure she'd go along with it first. I wanted Arial to love me, but it had to be natural and we weren't ready for that yet. We were on different paths right now and we were both young.

"OK Admiral Kingston, what have you got in mind for me?" I think she was catching on.

"I know you want to leave with your parents and my mom and dad, and perhaps it would be best for both of us if you do. I don't know what the future holds for the ship and crew, but I think you have a purpose with it."

She was waiting patiently. "Well, the Captains spot is already taken" she said.

"Yes, and he needs a great pilot and navigator. You've got the skills and I trust you as does the captain."

"Why do I sense a big but in the middle of this?"

I chuckled again. "Because I want you to come

back, and often." We turned and headed back to the house. Somehow we were holding hands.

"I suppose there's some great Earthling saying for what we have here?"

"There certainly is, if you truly love someone, you have to let them go."

"That's so silly" she giggled.

"Some people just call it hokey."

We kissed on the doorstep; then composed ourselves and walked into the house for supper. I announced that I had chosen the ships Pilot and Navigator. "Lieutenant Haldon! You will report to the captain immediately upon return to the ship."

She answered with a mischievous smile. "Aye, aye, Admiral Kingston."

Arson gave me the strangest look, I only smiled in return. I could see that wasn't what he had expected.

CHAPTER 64

Two days later they were ready to leave. Mom and dad had said their goodbyes to Dora and told her to mind her foster parents, study hard, and they'd be back before she could miss them. I used Ned's car to drive the six of us out to the farm. For convenience, it was late in the evening after the Farnham's kids were in bed and nobody would be likely to see the flyer as it left.

I pulled open the barn doors and Arial drove the big flyer out. I joined her inside while everyone else said their last goodbyes. It was quiet inside and we were temporarily alone. That was a new experience for both of us. I hated to see her go, but we both knew it was for the best for now. A quick kiss and then I left. The others boarded and shortly afterwards the flyer lifted off and was quickly gone from sight.

I sadly stood there and watched for it long after it had vanished from sight before turning to say good night to the Farnhams. They went back inside and I drove back to the house, tomorrow was going to be a busy day.

CHAPTER 65

That had been Monday evening, it was now Wednesday midafternoon. As I drove into the university parking lot, there was only one spot left over on the back side away from the dorm. I locked the van and walked down the hill to the admin office. Mrs. Stillwell had been glad to hear from me and I told her that it had taken longer than I had expected to clear up all of the family matters but things were well in hand now.

She sounded genuinely pleased and wanted to know if I would be returning soon.

"I'm not sure if I can catch up or not but I would be willing to try" I told her. "I haven't even had a chance to setup my schedule."

"Well don't you worry; I'll take care of it for you. But you first must come in and see me when you get here. When will you be arriving?"

"Is Wednesday too soon?"

"Sooner would be better, but Wednesday will have

to do. Remember, as soon as you get here!"

"Yes ma'am."

I couldn't believe how much paperwork was waiting for me. I had to sign for this thing and that thing. It was a good thing I already had most of my books and the parking sticker was already paid for. I grabbed my bags out of the back seat and hauled them and my books up to my third floor dorm room. I tried my key in the lock on the dorm room door; it still worked! Mrs. Stillwell had told me that no one else had been assigned to my room so it shouldn't have been disturbed.

It seemed like it had been years…well maybe only months since I had found Arial in here waiting for me. My mind flashed back to all that had happened in just this past week and a half. That was probably the biggest adventure anyone could ever experience in a lifetime. I decided against trying to catch the afternoon class, I'll catch up on Friday.

I gazed across at the empty side of the room. I wonder whatever happened to Jared. I had fully expected to see them show up to contest ownership of the Talisman. Did GraMorn deal with them? That was still a mystery I would probably never find the answer too. At least Arson was on the lookout for them.

Oh well, I have my own life to lead and started putting my things away. Books on the top shelf, clothes in the drawers under the bed, empty bags in the top of the closet, and the typewriter sits right there on the side table?

I had packed all of Jared's things in boxes and the custodian had picked the boxes up. I found Jared's note in his, now mine, van, and rushed back to retrieve the papers from one of the boxes. But the typewriter is still here? Come to think of it, I don't remember seeing it on the custodians cart, he must have thought it was mine. Oh well, I guess he has abandoned it.

The cover was held on by two buttons, one on each side. I popped the cover off and marveled again at the ancient seeming engineering of this simple machine. Let's see, paper goes in behind the roll, rotate the handles and it ratchets around to the front and behind this inked ribbon. Ah, this set of rollers holds the paper flat so that you can read it as you go. Press a key and this bar swings up with the matching letter striking the ribbon and leaving an inked image on the paper followed by the carriage moving to the left. I pushed a few keys and watched the letters form words upon the page.

I finally determined that the bar across the bottom just advanced the carriage to the left for the spaces. What should I write? I finally decided to write a note to Arial. I wouldn't be too personal, our relationship was going good right at the moment as I remembered the saying that Billy had told me just a few days ago about "Absence makes the heart grow fonder."

Hmmm, maybe I should wait a bit on that, let her

settle into her new job. I know eventually that the job title might rankle on her somewhat as it alluded to the fact that she now worked for me. I don't think that she has realized it yet and I'm glad I won't be near her when she figures it out.

I know! I'll write a letter to Jared thanking him for the van and the typewriter.

Dear Jared,

Just a quick note to thank you for the van. Doctor Stein said you wouldn't be coming back and had me pack your things. The custodian has stored them somewhere, but he overlooked the typewriter as it was still here when I returned, I hope you don't mind that I keep it for you.

Regards, Jason Kingston

I hit the paper advance once more and read the whole thing over. Maybe I should go down to the office in the morning and actually send this to him. That is if they know where he is. I thought about Arial again, I wonder if she misses me like I miss her? How could she have such an obnoxious cousin as Jared anyway?

"Whirrr!"

What is that? I searched the room before realizing that the sound was coming from the typewriter. I picked the machine up and looked underneath it. No, nothing there, but I could feel the machine softly whirring in my hands. I looked it over again, no wires and no cords.

Slowly I set it back down on the table top.

"Ding!" Then it started typing.

Message sent! Waiting for reply!

What the…!!!

"Ding!" and it started typing again.

Receiving message 1 of 1!

I quickly snatched the typewriter off the table and looked it over again; still no wires or cords. I hastily set it back on the table again just as it started typing again.

It finished the first line and the paper advanced twice.

My jaw must have hit the floor as I stared at what it had just written; No way!

HEY DUDE! How you been? Done anything exciting lately?

The end?